CONFESSIONS OF A HOLLYWOOD STAR

Dyan Sheldon is the author of many books for young people, including *Planet Janet, Planet Janet in Orbit, Sophie Pitt-Turnbull Discovers America* and *Confessions of a Teenage Drama Queen*, which was made into a major film. She has also written a number of stories for younger readers and adults. *Confessions of a Hollywood Star* is the third in the successful series that began with *Confessions of a Teenage Drama Queen* and *My Perfect Life*. Born in America, Dyan now lives in north London.

Books by the same author

CONFESSIONS of a HOLLYWOOD STAR

DYAN SHELDON

WALKER BOOKS
AND SUBSIDIARIES
LONDON · BOSTON · SYDNEY · AUCKLAND

First published 2005 by Walker Books Ltd
87 Vauxhall Walk, London SE11 5HJ

2 4 6 8 10 9 7 5 3 1

Text © 2005 Dyan Sheldon
Hollywood sign photograph © Beren Patterson/Alamy
All other photographs © Hemera Technologies/Alamy

The right of Dyan Sheldon to be identified as author of
this work has been asserted by her in accordance with the
Copyright, Designs and Patents Act 1988

This book has been typeset in Countryhouse and Sabon

Printed in Great Britain by Cox & Wyman Ltd,
Reading, Berkshire

British Library Cataloguing in Publication Data:
a catalogue record for this book
is available from the British Library

ISBN 1-84428-943-5

www.walkerbooks.co.uk

Move Over Scarlett Johansson, Here Comes Lola Cep

I was never really interested in being a movie star. Since I'm destined to be a great actor it's always been the theatre that held my heart in its noble and passionate grip. I longed to feel the ancient boards beneath my feet, to smell the greasepaint and hear the roar of the crowds – not compete with Mickey Mouse.

But life has a way of changing things, doesn't it? A person has to be flexible and willing to compromise when the Fates so decree. Face it – never doesn't mean *not ever* so much as it means *not until I have to*. So if Opportunity shows up in your front yard, you don't tell her to go away because she's wearing a Dior evening dress instead of Lady MacBeth's robes.

You say, "Come on in!" You say, "OK, maybe this wasn't exactly what I was planning, but it's a step in the right direction." (I mean, *eventually* I was going to do movies – after I established myself on the stage – so really what was the difference if I did it the other way round?)

Anyway, there was Opportunity, standing right in the middle of the lawn, but instead of coming in when I called her, she bolted. I couldn't believe it.

Luckily, like all great actors, I don't give up easily. I watched Opportunity run away – and then I chased after her.

Which is why I have a story to tell.

My Mother Strikes Another Blow For The Philistines

I was looking forward to graduating from high school the way Robinson Crusoe looked forward to getting off his island. Talk about dreams come true. As soon as it was over I would vacate my child's seat in the world's audience and my true life would finally begin! It was the moment I'd been planning from my first day in kindergarten. And since my mother had dragged me from the bright lights of New York City to the twilight zone of Dellwood, New Jersey, I had even more reason to look forward to the momentous day when I set out to seek my fortune in the real world. Not only would I finally escape the hopelessly dull tedium of my family, but the hopelessly dull tedium of suburban life as well. (Shakespeare's the only real connection I have with true passion since I moved here, but if you ask me even he would've been defeated by suburbia. Gone would be the stuff of true drama and he would've wound up with

Richard III standing in the supermarket offering his kingdom for a shopping trolley.)

I had everything figured out. Following in the footsteps of so many great thespians before me, I would study acting somewhere that pulsated with energy and creativity – a place who's spirit paid homage to the noble tradition from which it had sprung. Then I would wait tables (or possibly drive a cab) while I got whatever parts I could in serious plays performed in church halls and on the backs of trucks until I got my big break and made my (later to be legendary) Broadway debut. I couldn't wait. Just thinking about it made my blood bubble.

My first choice of drama school was the Royal Academy of Dramatic Arts in England (known to its intimates as RADA). I didn't really consider it a choice. I mean, just think about it. England is the birthplace of Shakespeare, Laurence Olivier, Dame Judy Dench and George Bernard Shaw (to name but a paltry few). And though I know that theatre started in Greece, it's pretty obvious that it would have started in England if England had been more than a few druids painting themselves blue at the time.

And RADA's in London, which is the cultural capital of the Old World. I ask you: is there a single great actor who hasn't performed there? A single major writer, poet, playwright or artist who hasn't at least visited? The answer is a resounding NO! Say what you will about the Old World, I think history is exciting. The streets of London are filled with plaques that mark the passing of the burning stars who have lit the darkness of human dullness and ordinariness for centuries. You know, Charles Dickens lived in a house on this site ... Oscar Wilde was arrested in this building ... Richard Burton passed out in this pub...

I mean, where else would a serious actor destined for immortality go to study her art but London, England?

I was still waiting to hear if I'd been accepted or not when my mother decided to tell me where else I could study. According to Karen Kapok, the serious actor destined for immortality would go to Brooklyn.

Of course I've always known that my mother's soul is as pedestrian as a pavement (she's a potter for God's sake, her life is all about mud), but this shocked even me.

"Brooklyn?" I cried. [Cue: rolling of eyes and moan of disbelief.] "You can't be serious." I'd applied to Brooklyn because she made me, but I thought it was just a fail-safe. You know, in case the wicked Princess Carla Santini cast a spell on me and I didn't get into RADA after all. "I'm not planning on a career in Mafia movies you know. I want to play Hamlet and Lear."

"As far as I can tell, you play Hamlet and Lear every day of your life," said my mother. "And I told you right from the start not to bother applying to RADA, didn't I?"

Did she?

11

Since it's not the kind of thing you could expect her to know, I explained that although the creative soul can survive without privacy or new clothes or its own phone, it cannot survive without spiritual nourishment.

"London is to the creative soul what a six-course dinner is to a starving man. Brooklyn's more like a McDonald's Happy Meal – and we all know how much nourishment's in that."

"You can forget the histrionics," said Karen Kapok. "You're not going to London. We can't afford it."

Like Life, true genius requires flexibility of course (you can't always get the lead, sometimes you have to accept a small, supporting role and make it big), so I was ready to compromise.

"OK," I said. "I'm willing to go to LA instead. Maybe they take late appli—"

"LA?" My mother has a very irritating laugh – something the twins have inherited from her. "I thought LA was a crass, materialistic, spiritual waste-land run by Satan wearing Mickey Mouse ears."

It never ceases to amaze me how a woman who can't remember to shave her legs more than once a year can remember practically every word I ever said and throw it back in my face.

"I may have said something like that once," I replied coolly, "but you're taking it out of context as usual. And anyway, I've revised my opinion since then. Many truly great actors have worked in Hollywood."

Karen Kapok proceeded to grind my hopes and dreams under her clay-covered foot. "But you're not going to be one of them. Brooklyn College has a perfectly good theatre department, and that's where you're going."

"Perfectly good for what?" I demanded. "Ralph Fiennes, Dame Diana Rigg, Sir Anthony Hopkins and Kenneth Branagh all studied at RADA. Name me one actor of any renown who studied in Brooklyn!"

"Dominic Chianese," said my mother.

As you can imagine, I said, "Who?"

"Dominic Chianese. He was Uncle Junior in *The Sopranos*."

Oh ye gods! And to think that my being related to this woman depended on one infinitesimal sperm being a good swimmer. It really makes you think.

"Well there you are!" My laugh was as bitter as bile. "Eat your heart out Ralph Fiennes! You can't compete with Uncle Junior."

Being a potter, Karen Kapok is a major aficionada of the obvious. "He's an actor," said my mother.

I reminded her that he's an actor who didn't work until he was in his seventies. "Do you expect me to wait over fifty years to get a job?" I demanded.

"What I expect is for you to go to Brooklyn College and live with your dad during the week, that's what I expect." She was in her Martin

Luther King we-shall-not-be-moved mode. "It's all arranged."

"Without consulting me of course!" I wailed. "After all, why should you consult me? It's only my life you're destroying. It's only my career that you're shredding into tiny pieces and sprinkling all over the grimy streets of Flatbush!"

"I'm glad that's settled," said my mother.

Let's face it: this is a world where one person's tragedy is another person's good fortune. There are women and children in Africa who have to walk six miles a day for polluted drinking water. You can't call them happy. But the men who are responsible for this long walk to get cholera are happy. Their factories are making so much money they can buy twelve-thousand-dollar showers and four-hundred-dollar bottles of wine.

And so it was for me with this cruel blow to my young dreams. Not everyone was as devastated as I was by this tragic turn of events.

Ella, for one, was ecstatic.

"But that's fantastic. I'll be practically right around the corner from your dad's." Ella was going to NYU. She hugged herself the way she does when she's really happy. "We can hang out just like always."

I don't want you to think that being able to see the best friend I've ever had every day didn't make me happy too. It made me happy. But not as happy as studying at RADA would have made me.

"Thanks," snapped Ella. "I'm so glad you value our friendship as much as I do."

"Don't be so melodramatic. Of course I value our friendship. But our friendship will endure the trials of time and distance. Whereas I may not be able to endure four years in a city whose only claims to fame are a baseball team that moved to California and a bridge."

"Woody Allen was born in Brooklyn," said Ella. "And Barbara Streissand."

I know she was trying to console me, but it was like throwing a drowning woman a feather.

"So what? I bet they left the first chance they got."

The other person who wasn't devastated that I couldn't *cross* the continent, never mind leave it, was Sam.

Sam wasn't going anywhere after graduation. He was staying in Deadwood and working at his dad's garage (which is pretty much what he's done his whole life; he's a genius when it comes to the internal combustion engine). Sam says he doesn't need to go to school to read a book or learn something new, which in his case is true. He's very self-motivated. And he doesn't like institutionalized education. He says it doesn't teach you to think, just to memorize.

"Brooklyn?" Sam whooped. "But that's great. It's practically next door."

As the Karmann Ghia flies.

I felt like tearing out my heart – or at least my hair. "It may have escaped your notice, but proximity to New Jersey isn't actually a guarantee of excitement, culture, or intellectual and spiritual stimulation."

"No, but it means I can come and pick you up on Fridays." He turned his attention to the toe of his boot. "I don't like the idea of you going thousands of miles away. I could die of boredom."

I clasped my heart. "Why Sam Creek – I didn't know you cared!"

He looked up. "Yes, you did. What I'm trying to figure out is if it's mutual, or if I'm all alone at the bus stop in the middle of the night and it's raining."

"Of course I care." This is true. The only fault Sam has is that my parents like him. "But you know I'm not ready for a serious relationship. Not until my career is on its way. Until then, I have to think of myself as going steady with my art."

"Well I like it better if you're going steady with your art in Brooklyn rather than England or LA."

I, Lola Elizabeth Cep (or possibly Sep – I still haven't decided which would look better in lights), do have a very resilient nature of course (as all true actors must). I wasn't going to let this tragic injustice ruin the end of my senior year. After all, I was still getting out of Deadwood, New Jersey, Carla Santini Capital of the World; I was still crossing the threshold of womanhood; and I was

16

still going to pursue my heart's passion, even if it was among people who say "tamayda" and not "toemahtoe".

I put my disappointment behind me and threw myself into the end of high school life with my usual high spirits and enthusiasm. I am, of course, destined to be one of the truly great actors, so it's no surprise that I convinced everyone that I didn't have a care in the world.

Even Mrs Baggoli, the drama coach, who was the only person besides Ella and Sam that I told about being sent to Brooklyn like prisoners used to be sent to Australia, was fooled by my performance.

"I must say, Lola, you're taking not going to RADA very well," said Mrs Baggoli. "After all I heard about it, I was expecting a few weeks of Meryl Streep in tears at the very least."

"The world isn't fair, Mrs Baggoli." I sighed philosophically. "But whatever the slings and arrows of outrageous fortune, the show must go on, mustn't it? In life as on Broadway."

Mrs Baggoli said I was very mature.

I was so good that I even convinced myself. Right up to a week before the end of classes, when I was suddenly reminded that though the gods have given me talent and dedication, they've always been pretty stingy with everything else.

It was Carla Santini who reminded me. Of course.

Carla Santini Reminds Me That I Wasn't At The Head Of The Line When The Gods Were Handing Out Luck

"Approximately one-hundred-and-sixty-eight hours and counting," hooted Sam. "Now, that's what I call getting seriously short."

"I don't know..." Ella shrugged. "It feels really strange thinking that after a few more days we'll never come here again."

Obviously I didn't actually feel like that myself, but my actor's brain totally understood what Ella meant. "Oh, I know, I know!" I cried, casting my arms wide to embrace the infinite mysteries of the universe. "The years of toil and struggle... The moments of dark heartbreak and the moments of pure joy... The days of laughter and of tears..."

"Well, not exactly..." Ella scrunched up her nose as though a bug had flown into it. "I just meant, you know, that we've been here a long time."

"Well of course we have." To me it felt like about a hundred years of hard labour. "There isn't an inch of this school that doesn't hold a memory."

"Tell me about it." Sam started ticking things off on his fingers (a habit he's developed through being a mechanic and having to tell people what's wrong with their cars). "The time you pretended to faint so you could get out of maths... The time you told Mrs Baggoli you didn't have your homework because you were chased by wild dogs... The time you ran me and Ella for class office without telling us... The time you got me to steal Eliza Doolittle's dress from the drama department..."

Like many people, Sam has a very selective memory.

"What about the time Carla Santini stopped the whole school from talking to me and Ella?" I didn't see why all the memories had to be of things I did. "Or the time she practically had me kidnapped? Or the time she told everyone you'd been in jail? And all the times she called me a liar when I was telling the total and absolute truth..." Several good reasons why, unlike Ella, I felt not nostalgia's cloying grasp for life at Deadwood High. "Which is why I can't wait to get out of here." To be honest, Carla had been so occupied with her graduation (so much bigger, better and more important than anyone else's) and everything related to it for the last month or so that she'd been almost civil to me recently (which means that she pretty much ignored me). I wanted to end on that high note.

19

This, however, was not to be.

Towards the end of lunch, Carla's voice, which had been playing in the background like musak all period, picked up volume and set the lunch trays trembling.

"Oh my God! I can't believe it! I had so much on my mind that I totally forgot to tell you what Daddy's giving me for a graduation present besides the new car."

Technically, this statement was made for the benefit of Carla Santini's disciples, Alma Vitters, Marcia Conroy and Tina Cherry. Carla, however, is excruciatingly generous when it comes to sharing her incredible good fortune with lesser beings, so there was no one in the cafeteria who wasn't under a headset who didn't hear her.

"Oh, God..." groaned Ella. "Not more good news."

I bit into a carrot stick. "Let's hope he's sending her to Mars. The first Princess on the Red Planet."

Sadly, it wasn't on a trip to Mars that Mr Santini was sending his only child. It was on a trip to the great continent of Europe.

"Stands to reason," muttered Sam. "They don't have any designer stores on Mars."

"Europe!" enthused Alma. "I've always wanted to go to Europe. It's so old."

"Me, too," chimed in Tina. "Continental men are supposed to be so much more romantic and sophisticated than American men."

Over the years of being a disciple of the Great

Santini, Marcia has perfected the envious but admiring sigh. "Oh my God, Carla... You are soo lucky!"

"Oh, I know I am..." It was pretty obvious from Carla's tone that she didn't think luck had anything to do with it. Without raising my head I could see the Santini curls swipe the air and those Bambi eyes glance over at me – as though by accident. "I mean, some people have to work all summer at a boring, meaningless job while I get to travel all over Europe practically free because Mommy and Daddy have so many connections." [Cue: pause for really enormous smile touched very lightly with humility.] "It really doesn't seem fair."

It didn't seem fair to me, either.

Though, of course, I pretended not to hear any of this. I know some people (like Karen Kapok and Mrs Baggoli) say that I exaggerate everything, but it's no exaggeration when I say that Carla Santini has been my nemesis since I first arrived in the soporific suburbs of The Garden State (so called because most life forms in New Jersey are vegetal). Carla is to Dellwood what the Queen is to England, only Carla's more attractive, dresses better and has more power than the Queen. For months after she got into Harvard the entire student body of Deadwood High had been bored to their bone marrow by Carla's tales of what going to an Ivy League school meant (apparently half the rulers of the world went to Harvard, which doesn't give us much hope for the future if you ask me) and what a great time she was going to have. That scintillating topic of conversation was finally shelved in favour of the car her parents were giving her as a graduation present (a silver, convertible Jag).

This, however, was one of those times when Carla wasn't going to let me ignore her.

"What do you think, Lola?" she roared from the next table. "If I have to choose a city to leave out of my itinerary, which should it be?"

I finally looked up, the smile of a Renaissance cherub on my lips. "You definitely don't want to miss Bucharest, Carla. It's very near Dracula's Castle."

Ella buried her face in her lunch and Sam choked.

Carla was amused. "No, really," she went on when she'd finished tittering inanely, "you're not like the rest of us provincials, are you? You're a cosmopolitan, cultured person. I'd really value your opinion."

Ella suddenly glanced at her watch. "God, would you look at the time?" Then she turned to me. "Didn't you want to go to the library before your next class?"

I wasn't the only one counting the days till I lived in a Carla-free world. Under my tutelage, Ella had gotten much better at confrontations, but hers is basically a placid nature and she still tended to shy away from actual hand-to-hand combat with

22

the Santini whenever possible.

Carla, of course, was going on as though Ella's words were no more than the rustle of a slight breeze. "I mean, I don't even have two whole months, do I? I mean, I have to have time when I get back to get ready for Harvard, so I'm just not going to be able to fit everything in."

"It kind of puts the problem of achieving world peace in a new perspective, doesn't it?" I asked.

Carla's smile flashed like a stiletto. "Oh I know it's not a huge deal really, but it's not something *you* have to worry about, is it?"

Since someone in the complex Dellwood, New Jersey spy network had obviously told her I already had a summer job, I wasn't sure where this conversation was leading – but it was unlikely to be somewhere I'd like.

"You mean because I have to work this summer?"

"Of course not." [Cue: clap hand over mouth and widen eyes in horrified realization of an innocent remark taken wrongly.] "Oh, Lola, you didn't think I meant *that*, did you? No, I'm talking about you going to study at RADA. What's a few measly weeks in Europe to someone who's actually going to live in England? Just think of all the great artists and writers and musicians RADA's produced." I could feel my own words being thrown back at me like peanut shells. "I mean, like just everybody, right? And you'll be in the same country where Shakespeare was born! Imagine

23

being able to walk in his footsteps!" She was in full-steam-ahead mode. I don't think she was even breathing. "And London! London, Lola! I mean, London's the cultural capital of the Old World, isn't it?"

"Ouch," I heard Sam mutter under his breath.

Ella started getting her things together. "We'd better get a move on, Lola, or we won't have enough time."

"You are still going to RADA, aren't you?" Carla's eyebrows (perfect to match the rest of her) were drawn together with concern, and her big, innocent eyes were on me like lasers. "Don't tell me you didn't get in?"

She knew I wasn't going. Was there no piece of private, personal information that she didn't know? I can understand why some people don't believe in God, but if you know Carla Santini you have to believe in the devil.

I raised my chin and the wattage of my smile. "Of course I got in." At least I would have if I hadn't cancelled my application.

"Oh, that's a relief." I've heard Carla's laugh described as the tinkling of glass bells in the mountains (by some besotted fool), but it always reminded me of bones being rattled in a jam jar (the bones of her victims). "Then you are still going. I mean, you have to still be going. I mean, we've been listening to you talk about RADA for months, haven't we?"

Programmed to respond like a NASA computer,

Tina, Alma and Marcia all nodded and hummed in agreement. *Forget the rack and thumbscrews*, their simpering smiles seemed to be saying. *We know what true torture is.*

Carla definitely knew about my not going to RADA because my mother's both impoverished and stubborn. Say what you will about phenomenally well-off, career-less women with nothing to do but play golf and eat lunch for charity, the Mothers of the Dellwood Spy Network outclass the FBI and the CIA combined.

Although I was aware that at the far corners of the cafeteria some kids were eating and talking amongst themselves in a normal kind of way (you know, like people who live in a world where the sun doesn't have to ask Carla Santini if it's all right to shine), around us all was quiet and still. We had everybody's undivided attention. People can sense when a hunter's getting ready to make a kill.

I thought about lying. In a few days we'd all have gone our different ways, and even if everyone found out that the closest I was getting to London was Brooklyn it wouldn't matter. But I couldn't. Not just because I'd promised Ella (and I do try very hard to keep my promises if at all possible), but because I knew I'd get busted. Unlike the army, Carla Santini takes no prisoners.

[Cue: small, self-mocking smile.] "Well, as it happens I decided against RADA for now." My smile shimmered with a noble sadness. "There were some personal things I had to consider. No girl is an island, you know."

"Oh, Lola, poor you! After all your plans!" If you ask me, the big cats of the Serengeti should be watching wildlife documentaries about Carla Santini to get their hunting skills up to scratch. "I hope you're going somewhere just as good."

I figured she must have our house bugged. How else could she know where I was going?

"Oh, I am," I assured her.

Ella and Sam were already on their feet, and I stood up, too.

"LA?" purred Carla. "They do have some good drama programmes in California."

"No." I gathered up my things. "Not LA. I consider LA a spiritual wilderness, dedicated to only the pursuit of money and mediocrity. It's not where you go for serious stage acting."

Carla didn't get to be the centre of the universe by not being persistent. "Well where do you go for serious stage acting, then?" Seventeen years of expensive dental care flashed. She wanted to hear me say it.

I swung my book bag over my shoulder. "I'm going to Brooklyn, of course. Some of America's finest actors have gone there."

"You mean like that old guy in *The Sopranos*?"

I'm pretty sure Carla was howling with laughter, but I was making my exit and didn't look back to make sure.

It was enough to know that everyone else was howling with laughter.

At Last The Gods Buckle Under My Pleas And Cajoling

In my opinion, the last few days of high school should be a gay, light-hearted and frivolous time. All the cares and woes that have been one's companions over the last few years are now no more than fading memories and the heart is filled with excitement and hope. Or it would be if Carla Santini lived in Finland.

But Carla Santini doesn't live in Finland, and even though she never stopped talking about how much she had to do to get ready for her trip, she didn't stay at home and do it. Instead she haunted the halls of Dellwood High like a scare of ghosts. She was everywhere. No matter where I went, there she was – larger than life and a lot more perfect. Hers was the only voice you heard, droning on and on about her European Experience as though she was the first person ever to have one. Even when I was in the sanctuary of my own room, listening to my favourite music and imagining my

Broadway debut (I tended to skip the wilderness years of Brooklyn), I still saw that smug smile and heard that self-satisfied voice. I felt like I'd starved myself for days because I was going to have this fantastic banquet, and then, when I finally sat down to eat, there was a dead rabbit in the middle of the table. It drove me crazy.

By Friday night, when Sam, me, Ella and Morty Slater went to the movies, I was metaphorically bent under the burden of Carla Santini and her unending good fortune.

"What's wrong with you?" asked Sam as we left the Dellwood cinema. "You didn't laugh once."

What was wrong with me was Carla Santini. I felt like I was being punished (on top of not going to RADA and having to spend four years in a place that no cab driver in Manhattan can ever find).

"I can't laugh." I stopped in front of the snack bar, raising my arms to the unheedful gods. "I just don't understand what I could possibly have done in a previous existence to deserve my life."

"Well let's see," said Morty. "Maybe you drove millions of Jews, gypsies, socialists and homosexuals into the ovens of Nazi Germany. Or you made a fortune in the slave trade. Or starved the Cheyenne. Or assassinated Martin Luther King."

[Cue: look of pity reserved for those with unimaginative, literal minds.] "I don't think so, somehow."

"But since you're a part of the human race, technically you did," said Ella. She was thinking of studying philosophy.

"Maybe you just wouldn't shut up about Carla Santini for more than three-and-a-half minutes," suggested Sam.

I felt that was really unkind.

Sam moaned. "For Chrissake, Lola. Why can't you just let up on the Santini gas pedal a little? I don't know about Ella and Morty, but I can't wait till I never have to hear the name Carla Santini again."

[Cue: cold look and disdainful readjustment of backpack.] "Oh, I'm so sorry if I've been boring you, Mr Creek, but I'm afraid I don't do public humiliation very well."

"Well you should," said Morty. "It's happened enough times."

"Hahaha…"

"And anyway," said Sam, "except for me, Morty and Ella, the only people who give a rusted bolt where you go to school or what poor country gets stuck with Carla Santini for the summer are you and Carla. Everybody else's got their own life to worry about."

"Sam's right," chipped in Ella. "It really doesn't matter. This time next week it will all be behind us." She gave me a warm smile. "Don't you at least feel good that you told the truth in front of everyone the other day?"

The answer to that question was: not really. I felt good about not being caught in another lie in front of everyone, but I'd've preferred to have said

I was going to RADA and had everyone believe me.

"I guess so." We strolled through the doors and into the hot New Jersey night. "But I still don't think it's fair. I really wanted to end this phase of my life on a high note. Now it'll haunt me for ever that Carla won the last duel." I clutched my heart, my face bleak with pain, my eyes on the stars. "There is no balm in Gilead!" I intoned. "Years from now, when I'm accepting my New York Drama Critics' Award, surrounded by adoring fans and admirers, what should be the greatest evening of my life will be marred by the memory of Carla Santini, making a laughing stock of me to the very end."

Ella applauded. "RADA doesn't know what they're missing," she said.

A great actor has to have a very persevering nature to be able to withstand the long, dark years of poverty, struggle and tepid reviews. That's why I can sometimes be a little obsessive and single-minded. Which is why I was still bemoaning my unhappy fate as I biked to my job at the used clothes store, Second Best, the next morning.

I pedalled slowly. I was in a ruminative and reflective mood. Ella and Sam could say what they wanted, but the unfairness of the world still galled me.

Is it really all just luck? I wondered. *Is that what a person's life comes down to? Where she was born ... who she was born to...? If you're born with tons of money, good skin, a lot of hair and enough brains to take the frozen dinner out of the box before you put it in the oven – does that mean you can do and be and have whatever you want?*

I sat out two red lights mulling this over in my mind.

One thing was for sure. If Carla Santini had been born to some migrant worker eking out a living picking lettuce one season and grapes the next, she wouldn't be going to Europe or Harvard. On the other hand, she'd undoubtedly still be convinced that she was God's greatest achievement, and bossing everyone else around. That's her nature.

And it's my nature to make the best of things, no matter how much havoc Fate may be wreaking on my life. But I still couldn't help feeling that I deserved better. I definitely deserved to make my exit from Deadwood High with my head raised and cries of "Bravo!" following me as I left the stage, not jeers of laughter because I'd tripped over Carla Santini (standing in the limelight as usual) on my way off.

Mrs Magnolia was all in a twitter because I was a few minutes late and she had to get to the bank.

"Where were you?" She was flapping around like a frightened bird. "I thought you promised to be on time today."

"Oh, Mrs Magnolia," I cried. "I am so sorry." I like Mrs Magnolia, but I wasn't about to tell her the truth – that my soul was heavy with discontent and it affected my legs. Mrs Magnolia has a kind heart, but she was born and raised in New Jersey (and will obviously die there unless she's abducted by aliens and expires on her way to Alpha Centauri), so though her heart is kind, her soul is sadly unevolved. My soul is vast and ancient like the Grand Canyon, but Mrs Magnolia's soul is small and contemporary like a cell phone. "You won't believe what happened to me. I was riding along, hurrying to get here, when this car—"

Mrs Magnolia held up one hand. "Not now. I don't have time." She picked up her bag and came from behind the counter. "There's some new stock in the back you can start sorting through. I have a few errands to do after I go to the bank. Will you be all right by yourself?"

I'd been working part-time for over a month; you'd think she wouldn't have to ask any more. I gave her my most reassuring smile. "Do ducks swim?"

She eyed me over her glasses. "And if you do have a customer you won't try to discourage her from buying what she wants, right?"

"Right." Mrs Magnolia always said the same thing to me when she left me alone because of the time she overheard me telling someone that the pinky-purple trousers made her look like an uncooked turkey. "I'll put myself in the role of a director of a multinational company who always puts profits before principles."

Mrs Magnolia smiled in that dazed way of hers.

"Thank you. I'd appreciate that."

I made myself a cup of Red Zinger tea (to revitalize my mind and body after the long ride), and then I started sorting through the new stock. I made four piles: ladies', children's, men's, and clothes that would only be worn by women who didn't know there was a world outside of New Jersey. My personal cares and traumas faded as I became deeply immersed in my work. I studied each new item, thinking about where it had been and what it had seen. Had that yellow dress with the ruffles been to a wedding? Did it dance and laugh and drink champagne – or did it end up weeping in the bathroom because the love of its life had married someone else? What about those jeans with the butterfly appliqued on the back pocket? Did that butterfly get to soar, to camp in the foothills of the Andes or sail the Gulf of Mexico? Or did it go no further than the nearest party or football game? Even worse, did it stay in the house watching videos and waiting for the phone to ring?

I picked up a pair of practically new red shoes with rhinestones in the heels. I was wondering what they would say if they could talk when the bell over the door rang.

There were two women standing at the front of the store, just kind of eyeing the room the way a greenhorn might eye her first bison. They looked too cool to be actual customers. The younger one had lilac highlights in her blonde hair and was dressed in an arty-funky way (clashing colours and patterns and earrings made from pull tabs off cans), and the older one had dark, short, spiky hair and looked excruciatingly, expensively hip (silver and black). I figured they were lost. I couldn't think of any other reason why women like that would come into Second Best.

"Can I help you?" I smiled warmly so they knew they weren't in one of those small towns where everyone's psychotic.

"No, thanks." The older woman shook her platinum earrings. "We're just looking."

The younger one took a dress from the rack and eyed it with interest. I was about to point out that if she wore that it would make her look like her name was Ethel when I remembered Mrs Magnolia's stern words.

"OK." Normally I would never leave customers alone in the front of the store, but my sensitive actor's instincts told me that they were too well-dressed to be thieves. I pointed to the open doorway. "I'll be in the back if you need me."

I returned to my sorting and wondering about the secret lives of clothes. Fragments of their conversation drifted towards me. Apparently, they weren't lost. Apparently, they were actually staying in some B&B in the area. *He's got as much charm as a slug and the food's so last century, but at least she's letting us use the washing machine... What if we dye this purple or black...?* They seemed to be shopping for presents, because it was all, *What about this for the girl in the gift store...?*

What about that for the cook in the diner...? Isn't this perfect for Lucy's dream...?

And then the funky one shrieked, "Oh my God, Shona, is this shirt Bret's character, or have I gone insane?"

My head went up like a periscope. Bret's character? Did she say Bret's character? Did she say Lucy's dream? Suddenly, all was clear as a new pane of glass! They were talking about Bret Fork and Lucy Rio – two of the hottest young actors around. These weren't ordinary women shopping for presents; they had to be costume designers looking for stuff for a film. As I said, I had no real interest in working in movies (not till I'd established myself in the theatre and commanded the right kind of parts), but a great actor has to be open to everything, not just the things she cares about in her soul. There is nothing in human experience that isn't fuel to the creative furnace.

I strolled from the back, cloaking my curiosity in professional concern.

"I couldn't help overhearing..." I hesitated, not wanting to interfere, but wanting to give what aid and succour I could. "It sounds like you're looking for something specific." I smiled – shyly, modestly. In my experience, nothing breaks the ice with strangers faster than a laugh shared. "If I can be of some help – I know our inventory better than Robert DeNiro knows Martin Scorcese."

When she stopped laughing, the older one looked me up and down, and was obviously satisfied from my outfit (I'd been in a retro-hippie mood when I got dressed that morning – skirt made out of an old pair of jeans and tie-dyed T-shirt) that she could rely on my judgement.

"Well, as a matter of fact," she said, "we're going to be shooting a movie nearby and we're looking for some things – especially vintage clothes from the fifties."

My smile was brighter than a Klieg light.

"You've come to the right place," I said.

Hooray For Hollywood!

I made much better time getting home than I had getting to work, but of course I was a lot more motivated on my return journey. I had news I couldn't wait to tell.

"Hooray for Hollywood!" I sang as I flashed through the leafy, anodyne streets of suburbia. I was going to be in a movie. Obviously I knew I wasn't going to get a major part, but I'd been so totally helpful, charming and entertaining to Leslie and Shona that I felt confident that some small but not insignificant role would be mine. *You know,* they'd say to the director, *we met this amazing girl in the secondhand clothes store ... you've really got to meet her ... she has so much star potential!*

The lawn sprinklers waved at me like fans at the Oscars as I sped towards home. "Hooray for Hollywood!" Tinsel Town may have crushed the dreams of millions of starving would-be stars, but it was going to make at least one of my dreams come true: the one where Carla Santini ate sand.

My mother and the twins were in the kitchen when I arrived. I would have ignored them and gone straight to the phone to call Ella, since she's far more interested in my life than any of my relatives, but the domestic tableau that greeted me made me stop in surprise. Karen Kapok was at the stove, stirring like a witch at her cauldron, and Paula and Pam were mauling vegetables at the table.

"Good God!" I cried. "You're cooking! Don't tell me the President's coming for supper."

My mother glanced at me over her shoulder. "Actually, I thought Sam was coming for supper."

So much had happened today that I'd totally forgotten she'd invited him over for a meal to celebrate our graduation.

"Of course he is." I laughed as though I'd been joking.

Pam looked up from her attack on the spinach. "How could you forget that?" she demanded. (No prizes for guessing who she takes after.)

"As it happens," I said, "I've had other things on my mind: more exciting things than watching Sam see how many calories he can take in at one sitting."

Paula bit into the carrot she was supposed to be slicing for the salad. "Like what?"

I'm used to skepticism, ridicule and an appalling lack of interest from my family, but I was too excited to let this stop me from sharing my news.

38

I smiled in a casual, understated kind of way. "It just so happens that they're making a movie right here in Dellwood, that's what."

For once an announcement of mine actually got the right reaction from my sisters. They dropped their knives and vegetables and began jumping up and down.

"Really? A movie? Here?" shrieked Pam.

"Do you think they're looking for a set of twins?" Paula is by far the more practical of the two.

I said I'd see if I could put a good word in for them with the director.

Karen Kapok, immersed as she is in earth, asked, "And where did you hear this?"

I told her where I'd heard it.

"And what makes you think you'll get to put a good word in with the director?" asked my mother.

I explained that I was practically guaranteed a part. Which was more or less true. They'd said they knew the movie needed extras.

Karen Kapok did her impersonation of a refrigerator overworking. "Hmmm…"

"Hmmm…?" I echoed. "Hmmm, what?"

"I just don't think you should get your hopes up," said my mother. "There's no guarantee you'll get a part – even as an extra."

"Hope is the fuel of the ship of dreams," I informed her. "Without hope you can't even get out of the harbour. Besides, let's not forget that I do have inside connections."

Pam looked to my mother "What's that mean?"

"It means Mary sold the costume designers a bowling shirt," said my mother. My mother *will not* call me Lola, just because it isn't the name she gave me when I was born and too young to have an opinion.

"I should've known I wouldn't get any encouragement from you." I headed for the door. "I'm going to call Ella. At least she'll be glad for me."

"What happened to you?" asked Ella. "You're in a much better mood than you were last night."

I laughed. Last night was as far away from me by then as the Ring Nebula. "And how could I not be happy?" I demanded. "Don't I live in this glorious jewel of the crown of the State of New Jersey?"

"Are we talking about *Dellwood*?"

"Where else? Haven't I ever told you how much I love dear old Dellwood with every fibre of my being?"

"No," said Ella, "you haven't. You usually describe it as prison with its own shopping centre."

I disregarded the flat, sour tone in her voice. "Well I do love it. I love its quiet, tree-lined streets. I love its giant supermarkets. I love—"

Ella interrupted my flow. "Lola, is that really you?"

"Oh hahaha," I said. "I know that, in the past,

I have had one or two small criticisms to make of your home town, El, but now I'm ready to get down on my knees and thank the gods for bringing me here from the mean streets of Manhattan. Really. Just ask me how happy I am to be spending my summer here among the shopping centres and lawn sprinklers of Dellwood instead of some dreary, passé place like London or Paris or Rome. Just ask."

"How happy are you?" She asked this warily. Ella distrusts mood swings.

I was practically dancing I was so excited. "I'm happier than a million-dollar lottery winner. I'm happier than the champions of the Super Bowl. I'm happier—"

"Have you been drinking, Lola? Tell me the truth."

[Cue: heavy sighing and rolling of eyes at the calendar from the Chinese take-away on the wall. This month's sage advice was: *A wise man eats well and says little*.] "That really beggars belief, El. I mean, you of all people asking me that. You know what I think of the tragic destruction of lives by alcohol."

"My mo—"

"I wasn't thinking about your mother." Mrs Gerard has a problem with white wine (which is one of the reasons Ella distrusts mood swings). "I was thinking of actors like Anthony Hopkins and Dennis Quaid."

Ella said, "Oh."

A great actor has to be prepared for people who laugh at the wrong line or cough during Hamlet's soliloquy, so I wasn't discouraged by this detour in the conversation. My excitement was undiminished.

"Now can I tell you my totally awesome news?"

"OK," said Ella. "What happened?"

I told her about the costume designers coming into the store.

"Their names are Shona and Leslie, and they're working on this big Hollywood movie!"

"Really?" Ella sounded skeptical. "And they were shopping in Second Best? Why would they do that?"

"Authenticity. But that's not the best part," I assured her. "Wait till you hear. It stars Bret Fork and Lucy Rio. The movie's about a girl remarkably like me who is dragged away from her home and friends and everything she loves to live in a new town. But instead of being haunted by Carla Santini, she's haunted by the ghost of a fifties biker who doesn't want her and her family in his house."

"Oh my God! Are you sure?" At last she'd caught my excitement. "But this is incredible! A movie right here in Dellwood! I've always wanted to see a real movie set. Do you think they'll let people watch?"

Since I'd visited several streets that had been turned into movie sets when I lived in the civilized world, I was the expert. "Of course they will. They're filmmakers, aren't they? They love to be watched."

"Oh, Lola..." A new, truly awesome thought had occurred to Ella. "Wait till Carla hears about this. She's going to go incendiary when she finds out that something like this is going on while she's in Europe looking at old buildings."

I smiled into the receiver. "Especially when she finds out that I'm going to be in the movie."

Ella was raised to be ladylike and demure, but she can squeal like a litter of pigs when she wants to. "Go on! Are you serious? You got a part?"

"Well, as good as. I know for a fact that they'll be looking for extras." Not that I had any more intention of having a non-speaking part in a professional production than I do in life. "Of course I don't really think that being the back of a head in a crowd is compensation for not going to RADA," I went on, "but I'm confident that once they see me in action they'll find something more substantial for me."

Ella said, "Lola..."

"What?"

"Well..." I could hear Ella choosing her words as if they were chocolates. "I don't know if you should count on that..."

I told her she sounded like my mother. But I was in too good a mood to let the naysayers dampen my spirits. Right at the eleventh hour I was going to take my final revenge on Carla Santini for all the years of grief and humiliation she'd caused me. "And anyway," I continued, "the most important thing is that Carla will miss the whole thing." I laughed. "It

43

couldn't be better if I'd planned it myself."

In the few precious minutes of privacy and peace we had before the free-for-all otherwise known as supper with Karen Kapok and her younger daughters, I told Sam about the movie.

"I don't get it," said Sam. "So they're making some movie here. What's the big deal?"

"What's the big deal?"

"Yeah. I mean, it'll be good for the town – you know, for business – but except for that what's the big deal?" He gave me a searching look. "Oh, hang on. You want to be in this dumb movie. That's it, isn't it?"

"And what's wrong with that?" Considering how annoying Sam can be, it often amazes me how much I like him. "I am an actor, after all. It's not like being a mechanic. You can refuse to work on four-by-fours because you think they're nothing but gas-guzzling status symbols, but actors don't always have the luxury of being able to turn down jobs."

"Right," said Sam. "That's why all those big stars do those really crappy movies and commercials. Because they're afraid of starving to death."

"Whatever. I don't really want to have this argument right now." This is what I mean about being annoying. I'm all in favour of principles, of course, but Sam's inflexibility drives me nuts. "And anyway, that still doesn't mean it's not exciting.

Personally, I think it's the most exciting thing that's happened around here since the revolution."

"Oh yeah? Well, personally, I think making another mindless, shallow, meaningless movie isn't nearly as exciting as a populist revolt."

[Cue: the heartfelt sigh that can sometimes be the only communication between one parallel world and another – in this case the imaginative one of the artist and the practical one of the skilled craftsman.] "And how do you know this movie's going to be mindless, shallow and meaningless?"

"Well it's not going to be *Little Big Man* or *Catch-22*, is it?" Those are Sam's all-time favourite movies. "Not with those lame-os in it."

No one has ever accused Sam Creek of being starstruck.

I sighed again. "As you know very well, I think the only true drama takes place in the theatre – and of course I totally agree with you about a lot of the movies churned out by Hollywood, but let's not forget that the entertainment industry is very important to the economy. It makes billions of dollars a year."

"So does the arms trade but that doesn't mean it's a good thing."

"Oh, please... There's no comparison. People don't need to be shot or bombed, but they do need to be entertained. Man does not live by bread alone you know."

Sam put his how-could-you-forget-to-check-the-oil look on his face. "Baseball's entertaining.

So are basketball and soccer." He started ticking off all the things in the world that are more entertaining than movies. "And bowling. And gymnastics. And the flying Shalon monks. And ballroom dancing."

"Ballroom dancing?" I didn't even think Sam knew what ballroom dancing was.

"Yeah. Ballroom dancing."

"Are you saying that you watch ballroom dancing?"

"Sometimes. On cable. My dad likes it."

It's true that, no matter how old you get or how much you think you know, life always has another surprise waiting. "Your father likes ballroom dancing?"

"Yeah. He won trophies. That's how he hooked up with my mother."

I never met Sam's mother of course (she was killed in a car crash when Sam was four), but I have met Mr Creek. Mr Creek's a small, thin man who looks like a balding troll who fell into a grease pit. It was really difficult to picture him doing the Fandango in a powder-blue lycra jumpsuit covered with sequins. "*Your* father was a ballroom dancer?"

"You're repeating yourself."

"Just answer the question."

"You're not the only person who likes to show off, you know," said Sam.

I made a face. "I'm not saying I wouldn't like some minuscule part in this movie – if I can't go to

RADA I do feel it's the least I deserve – but for your information it just so happens that this isn't actually about me. It's about someone else in Deadwood who likes to show off."

A slow smile spread over his face. "We're talking about Carla, aren't we?"

"Who else?"

Carla thinks that when the Bard said *all the world's a stage* he meant her stage – and that everyone else is only here as her audience.

"Don't tell me you don't want to see her face when she finds out that Dellwood's being turned into a movie set while she's off shopping in Rome."

"Oh, now I get it." Sam laughed. "Now that's a hell of a lot more entertaining than baseball."

Like A Loaded Gun,
Improvisation Can Be A
Dangerous Thing

I chose my outfit carefully on Monday morning. I wanted something casual and understated to contrast with the importance of the part I was about to play (the triumph of Good over Evil). I finally decided on a pair of vintage, button-fly jeans, a white silk shirt and the rope and canvas sandals Cal brought me back from Spain (my father's picture books are very popular in the Old World). I thought of it as the Nicole-Kidman-goes-grocery-shopping look.

Because she never stops talking about herself, Carla Santini is the kind of person who constantly gives you the feeling of déjà vu. When Ella, Sam and I got to the cafeteria that afternoon she was still going on about her holiday as though about three minutes had passed, not three days. The disciples were gathered around her, listening raptly, for all the world as though they'd never heard any of it before either.

48

"Oh, Lola! There you are!" The gold bracelets on Carla's wrist jangled like alarm bells as she waved her hand in my direction. "I've been wanting to talk to you. I had this fantastic idea last night."

"Oh, really?" I stopped at the end of her table. I could hear Sam and Ella taking seats at the next one along. "What's that? You're leaving for Europe before graduation?"

Carla pouted as though her feelings were hurt (which is impossible since she doesn't have any).

"We only have five more days of school left, Lola," Carla informed me. "Don't you think we could finally call a truce? I for one bear no grudges." The curls shimmered. "And just to prove it, I want to do you a favour."

The only favour I wanted from Carla was for her to leave for Europe yesterday.

"A favour?" Was this a large, wooden horse being hauled through the gates of Troy by Gucci-clad Romans that I saw? "What kind of favour?"

"I thought I could bring you back something from London." Carla smiled at me like the Queen smiling on an African shaman who's showing her how to perform a rain dance. "You know, like a consolation prize for not being able to go yourself."

What a generous girl. She'll win the Nobel Peace Prize yet.

My laughter bubbled like Alka-Seltzer. "Oh, Carla," I gushed, "that is so incredibly kind of

49

you..." The shaman smiled back at the Queen. "But I wouldn't want you to go to any trouble for me. Especially when we all know how busy you're going to be." The shaman knew that a monsoon was about to hit, sweeping away the very piece of land on which the Queen was standing, and was pretty pleased with herself. "And anyway, it really isn't necessary. I'm happy to be able to say that the gods have already compensated me for my temporary disappointment."

Alma, Marcia and Tina all glanced at Carla, but Carla didn't blink. "Really?" One eyebrow rose like an inquisitive snake. "And how have they done that? Shut down Brooklyn College?"

"Oh, Carla ... you don't know how much I'm going to miss your sense of humour." To prove this, I gave a very good impersonation of the Santini laugh of tiny glass bells knocking against each other in a high wind. "But it's actually something that's happening right here in Dellwood."

"Here?" The disciples' eyes were flipping back and forth like tennis balls at Forest Hills, but Carla's eyes didn't move from mine. "In Dellwood? Don't tell me they're reopening the Red Barn Theatre and you've got a job as an usher."

The Red Barn Theatre was once suburban New Jersey's answer to The Globe. Every summer it would put on old Broadway plays performed by professional actors (though largely ones who were household names only in their own homes), but it

50

dropped its final curtain (though of course it didn't actually have curtains) before I got to town.

"Close." A warm feeling, almost of affection, towards Carla filled my heart. How was I ever going to find someone in the hometown of Walt Whitman and Junior's cheesecake who could replace her? "And it's almost as good."

"Well come on..." She exchanged smirks with Tina, Marcia and Alma. "Don't keep us in suspense."

"Well, you're not going to believe it," I leaned my arms on the plastic table top, making myself comfortable, "but it looks like they're going to be shooting a Hollywood movie right here in dear old Dellwood!"

A wave of excitement ran through the student sea – but failed to even lap at Carla's toes.

"Really?" Her smile was steady as concrete. "I didn't hear anything about this."

"No?" I shook my head sympathetically, baffled by a world that could behave so strangely.

"Well I do think that Daddy would've been told. He is one of the most important men in town."

"And don't I know it?" The only people who didn't know it were in the cemetery. "I guess your father was probably too busy buying you cars and trips to Europe to keep his eye on everything else in town." I gave her a consoling smile. "Anyway, I think they've just made their final decision, so they're probably sending him an urgent fax even as we speak."

51

Carla's lips were straight as a blade. "And just how do *you* have all this inside information?"

"She made it up like she usually does," muttered Tina.

I knew exactly what I was going to say, of course. It was short, but it was very sweet. I'd tell Carla about the costume designers coming into Second Best, and probably mention that I'd been more or less promised a job as an extra. But what I'd planned didn't include any extraneous details about what anyone else would say – or how they'd look. It definitely hadn't included the expression of disdainful skepticism on Carla's beautiful face, or the Greek chorus sighing and snuffling behind her. These changes required some adjustments. They required improvization. I've always been good at improvization.

"Me?" I straightened up, sidling slowly towards the empty seat next to Sam. "Oh, the director came into the store – you know, where I work?" Out of the corner of my eye I could see Ella staring at me, a sushi roll frozen between her lips, but my attention was on the scene in my mind of a man who looked a lot like Martin Scorcese striding through the door of Second Best. "He was checking out the location and everything. He wanted to know all about Dellwood and what was around..." I smiled fondly at the memory. "We had a really good talk."

"Oh, really?" Carla's voice was hard, but the practiced ear could hear the tiny wedge of doubt prising open the steel door of her confidence. "What about? Secondhand clothes?"

The disciples tittered.

"As a matter of fact we did touch on that topic. He was looking for vintage stuff for Bret. You know ... Bret Fork?" I pulled out the chair and sat down, looking over my shoulder at her. "But then – much to my astonishment – he wanted to know if I'd ever done any acting myself." I laughed with surprised delight. "Can you imagine?"

I couldn't see Ella even out of the corner of my eye now, but I could hear her. She sounded like someone had just punched her in the stomach.

"Oh, please..." [Cue: long-suffering sigh.] "Why would he ask you that?"

"Because he liked my face." I didn't even have to pause to think. It was like I was reading from a teleprompter. "He said he was looking for someone with my combination of wholesomeness and sophistication."

"Oh, God..." groaned Alma, Marcia and Tina.

"You'll be telling us you got the lead next," Carla snickered.

"No, not the lead." I stared into her eyes like I was trying to read something behind her head. "It's nothing big of course – just one of those blink-and-you-miss-it kind of parts really – but it should be fun."

Carla didn't say anything. She suddenly had to go. "I'll see you later," she informed the disciples. "I just remembered I have something to do."

53

She marched out of the cafeteria the way Pinochet's troops marched into Santiago.

Ella finally dropped her sushi roll. "Are you crazy?" she hissed. "Why did you tell her you had a part?"

"She goaded me into it." I opened my lunch box. "And anyway, what's it matter? Friday's our last day of school."

"Thank God this part of our lives is almost over," muttered Sam.

Sadly, he has no future as a prophet.

Carla Beats Defeat To The Ground And Snatches Victory Out Of Its Jaws

It was a Dellwood High tradition that on the last day the senior class threw a barbecue for the other years. Since there was no school social event that wasn't taken over by Carla Santini I planned to miss it. But Sam and Ella wanted to go, and because Morty was senior class president and put soya burgers on the menu I couldn't even argue that a vegetarian at a barbecue is like a teetotaller at a drunken Harvard student party (offended and bored), so I let myself be persuaded.

The barbecue was a happy, jubilant affair. There was a lot of last-minute yearbook signing, and a lot of stories that began with "Remember the time...?" and ended in hysterical laughter. A surprisingly large number of the "Remember the time" stories concerned me.

"Well you can't say you haven't made a big impression on this school," said Ella.

Sam put an arm around my shoulders. "Nobody's

going to forget you in a hurry."

I smiled, but not with the completely unbridled enthusiasm you might have expected. It was always my intention to make a big impression on the student body of Deadwood High, of course, but what I wanted was to be a symbol of the great world beyond the golf course and three-car garages. An inspiration! A living legend! Years from now, when these same callow youths were wrinkled and grey, I wanted them to say, "Lola Cep was one of the biggest influences on my formative years. She opened my eyes to the glories of the universe." Not, "I'll never forget Lola Cep. What a character – she gave us a lot of laughs."

But this moment of gloom passed quickly. After all, I wasn't exactly finished, was I? I hadn't even begun.

"They're not going to have a chance to forget me. Someday the whole world will know who I am." I squared my shoulders and smiled into the clouds. "But right now it's time for me to bid my teary adieus to the Wicked Witch of the East."

Sam groaned. "I thought that was all over."

There wouldn't be any opportunity for schmoozing at the graduation on Sunday and I wanted to say one last fond farewell to Carla before our paths parted for ever (it was like touching the corpse of your enemy to make sure she's really dead). Also, I figured that a public bon voyage would dispel any lingering doubts that I'd been lying about the movie.

"It is all over," I assured him. "I just want that feeling of closure."

"I have a feeling of closure," said Sam. "I threw out all my notebooks last night."

I took Ella by the arm. "Come on. It'll only take a minute."

"And then it'll finally be over, right?" Sam insisted. "No more Carla this and Carla that. You're never going to say her name again."

"Never," I promised. "Not even instead of swearing."

And I meant it. I know I sometimes exaggerate a little for dramatic effect, but I sincerely believe that in all serious matters a person's word should be her bond. This was to be the last scene Carla and I ever played together.

I would find Carla among the revellers. I'd go up to her all smiles and girlish gushing. A hush would fall around us. This was as historic a moment as Roosevelt meeting with Stalin or Tom Cruise and Nicole getting divorced. I'd say I hoped she'd have a great time running Europe. Carla would promise to give my regards to London. Then, just as I was about to turn away I'd make a joke. "Who knows?" I'd say. "Maybe the next time you see me will be in the movies..."

Carla was holding court on the lawn outside the library, surrounded by the usual suspects (Tina, Marcia and Alma) and a gaggle of lesser hangers-on.

"Carla!" I cried as Ella and I drew near. "I just wanted to wish you bon voyage! Have a great time

57

in Europe. Do give it my love."

The disadvantage of real life as opposed to a play is, of course, that not everyone's working from the same script. So although I knew exactly how this scene was supposed to go, it wasn't how Carla read it.

"Oh, haven't you heard?" Carla's smile was shy and perplexed.

The disciples were all smiling, too, but their smiles were expectant. They knew there was a banana skin right in front of my feet.

"Heard what?"

"I'm not going after all."

Beside me, Ella whispered, "Oh God... I should've known."

If you ask me, human nature could use some improving. History repeats itself over and over, yet people are always surprised when there's another war, or another famine, or another politician is caught lying. Just like I was surprised by Carla Santini pulling a Carla Santini at the last minute. Ella was right: I should've known.

"You what?"

"There's been a change of plan." Carla tossed her shining, healthy hair and beamed. "I'm not going to Europe. Not this summer anyway."

"But you can't be serious!" Sincerity lent a certain poignancy to my performance. "You were so excited..." I don't like to wish ill on anyone of course – it's really incredibly bad for your karma – but I couldn't help hoping that the reason for this tragic turn of events was something truly serious. Like that Mr Santini'd been arrested for fraud or that Mrs Santini'd run off with the gardener.

"Oh, I know." Carla sighed as though she had personal experience of disappointment. "I'm devastated of course. Totally devastated. But what can you do?" If the Dalai Lama had caught her laid-back, understanding smile he would've thought he had a follower. "Things happen, don't they?"

Tina, Alma and Marcia all murmured sympathetically.

"So what went wrong?" Things definitely happen to me, and most of them are bad.

But only good things happen to Carla Santini.

"Oh nothing went wrong really." She shrugged and smiled almost shyly. "It's Daddy. As soon as he heard about the movie he insisted on finding out all about it."

So that was why Carla left the cafeteria so abruptly; she wanted to call Daddy on her cell phone.

"You know what he's like," said Carla.

Do I know my own name? Mr Santini is Carla's father after all. You don't get lemons from an apple tree, do you? And I know Carla, too. If my mother could manipulate clay the way Carla manipulates Mr Santini, our name would be Wedgwood.

Carla steamed on, not expecting an answer. "So, can you believe it, it turns out that Daddy knows the director, Charley Hottle. Isn't that some coincidence?" She paused so everyone – especially

I – would know it wasn't a coincidence. It was because Mr Santini knows everybody, unless, of course, they aren't rich or famous and therefore not worth knowing. "You've heard of Charley Hottle, haven't you?" crooned Carla.

There might be a small community of Innuit out on an ice floe somewhere who hadn't heard of Charley Hottle, but everyone else with electricity, newspapers and magazines knew who he was. He was one of the biggest directors around, known as much for his fervent belief in family values (he had seven children and just the one wife) as for his films. Charley Hottle's movies contained no sex, no violence and no dangerous ideas. He loved ordinary people and the simple life. Which didn't explain how he got to be a pal of Mr Santini's.

Carla gave a girlish gasp. "Oh, how silly of me. Of course you know who he is. You've already met him, haven't you?" The disciples snickered in a discreet, ladylike way, but Carla gave me the smile that's been known to blind strong men. "Well of course they got talking and you know how generous Daddy is. He offered Charley the use of the cottage out back – you know, in case he or Bret and Lucy don't want to camp out in a trailer or whatever it is they usually do."

The Santinis' "cottage" only fits that description if you're comparing it to a palace.

"Your father's practically a saint," I muttered. The saint of spoiled brats.

Carla shrugged in the philosophical way of

princesses throughout the ages. "So I can't possibly leave my parents at a time like this, can I?"

Marcia, Alma and Tina all shook their heads – sadly. They didn't think she could possibly leave the Santinis at a time like this either.

"I mean, it's too much to expect them to cope with actors and a film crew all on their own." She sighed. "Everybody knows how I was looking forward to seeing the Sistine Chapel and shopping along the banks of the Seine and everything, but sometimes you just have to put yourself second, don't you?" She was looking straight at me of course.

I smiled in the philosophical way of servants throughout the ages. "Well, Europe's waited centuries for you to visit – I guess it can survive a little longer."

I could tell from the faces of the disciples that I hadn't yet stepped on the banana skin. But I was about to.

The tiny glass bells tinkled wildly. "Naturally, Daddy found a way to make it up to me."

I didn't reply. I felt like someone tied to a stake watching a rhino charge towards her. I knew what was going to happen next.

Carla's smile was so out of control by now that I felt like I was staring right at the sun. "Can you believe it? He asked Charley if maybe they could find a small part in the movie for me, and Charley was so grateful that he said yes!"

I could believe it. What I couldn't believe was that this was all my fault – me and my big mouth.

"Isn't that awesome?" breathed Marcia.

"Awesome..." echoed Tina.

"Awesome..." echoed Alma.

"Well, I couldn't refuse, could I?" purred Carla.

I forced myself to rally. "Of course you couldn't. You have too generous a nature."

Carla's voice was like cream sliding over ice. "So I guess I'll see you on set," said Carla.

"If Lola really has a part, you mean," said Alma. Tina nodded.

Marcia said, "That's right. Just because Lola says something doesn't mean it's true."

They must've rehearsed this at least a dozen times. They all had their parts down pat.

I smiled back. "Don't worry," I said. "It's true."

"And we've heard that before," said Tina.

Once again I made my exit not to applause, but to laughter.

If you believe what you read on greetings cards and in magazines, the benefit of friends is having people around who comfort and support you when the cold, cruel world turns against you and your soul has more dark nights than the army has guns. "I am lost!" you cry to the uncaring sky. "How can I hope to go on?!" And that's when your friends all rally round, telling you how great you are and how none of your problems are your fault.

I was totally in an *I am lost! How can I hope to go on?* mood after my conversation with Carla.

"I can't believe it," I muttered as Sam, Morty,

Ella and I climbed into Sam's car. "Carla always gets her way. She must've been an absolute monarch in a previous life." Either that or God.

As an example of how real life does not imitate greetings cards, Ella said, "Just forget it, will you?"

Sam was even more sympathetic. He looked at me like I was a leaking carburetor. "It serves you right," said Sam. "That's what you get for lying."

Even Morty jumped on the I-told-you-so wagon. "You really should've known this would happen," said Morty. "It's not as if you don't know what she's like."

"I know she's a devious, egocentric, manipulative witch, but even I didn't expect her to dump Europe for this."

Sam looked over at me as we moved out of the parking lot. "Why not?"

"Because I didn't, that's why not."

"You're like a kid playing with a loaded gun who's all surprised when he shoots himself with it," said Sam.

"I begged you not to lie any more, didn't I?" chimed in Ella. "I don't know why you can never just let sleeping dogs snore away in the corner. Why do you always have to wake them up?"

Has anyone been more misunderstood than I? "But that's exactly the point!" I wailed. "I wasn't lying, was I?"

Sam's a very conscientious driver, but even he took his eyes from the road for a second to look at me. "What do you mean you weren't lying?"

63

"You mean you really got a part?" demanded Ella. Since everything in Sam's car is no more than a few inches away she was pretty much screaming in my ear.

"Not exactly. I mean, not yet. But I will. That's why it wasn't a lie. It was just a premature announcement."

Sam hooted. "A premature announcement? Is that like a pre-emptive strike?"

"And just how do you intend to get a part?" bellowed Ella. "Are you planning to ask Mr Santini if he can pull some strings?"

[Cue: sigh of infinite patience being shoved over the edge.] "I told you. Those women I met said all I had to do to be an extra was turn up on the first day of shooting."

"You and half the town," said Morty. "Unless they're redoing Spartacus or something and need some really big crowd scenes, you're going to have to line up now."

But mine of course is an optimistic nature. "I'm sure I'll get something," I assured him. "I do have experience."

"All this is beside the point," cut in Sam. "It may have slipped your mind, Ms Cep, but the Carla Santini phase of your life's supposed to be over, remember?"

"It's not over till the final curtain."

"This was the final curtain," Sam informed me.

I smiled to myself. That's what he thought.

Predictable As Always, The Gods Turn Against Me Again

Graduation was on Sunday, and on Saturday my father and his dog came out from the city to join in the celebrations so I had no chance that weekend to do anything about furthering my movie career.

I had a restless, brooding two days. Morty, with his logical, mathematical mind was right. Now that Carla was not only in the movie but practically living with the stars, the word was out, spreading through the leafy streets of Dellwood like fire across the Californian forests. There were going to be enough hopeful extras in Dellwood to film every epic ever made (all at the same time), and a lot of those hopefuls were going to be friends of Carla Santini – which meant that they were more shoe-ins than hopefuls. My only chance was to get there first. Which meant before the shooting started. If I could find Shona and Leslie and remind them that they more or less promised me a part, all my problems would be over. I didn't figure that would be too hard.

Even though I didn't have to be at Second Best until one on Monday, I got up practically at the crack of dawn. My mother, who has a very opportunistic nature, wanted me to take the twins to day camp for her since I had "time to kill", but I said that I couldn't even injure time, I was meeting Ella. This was more or less true. I would be meeting Ella, she just didn't know it yet. She'd been busy with her family all weekend, too, so I hadn't had a chance to tell her.

Karen Kapok gave me one of her is-this-bowl-off-centre looks. "So early? What are you doing, going fishing?"

I never like to tell my mother my plans if I can help it in case she tries to stop me. I said we had a lot to do before I went to work.

As soon as my mother and the twins left for the day camp, I called Ella.

"What time is it?" She sounded semi-conscious.

"You don't want to sleep your life away," I told her. "The early actor catches the part."

Ella wanted to know what I was talking about. I told her my idea.

"You want to do *what*?"

"It's my only chance. They liked me. They said all I had to do was turn up. I'm sure if I explain to them the urgency of the situation, they can fix it so I don't have to mill around in the street with the rest of the town."

Because I don't want to miss so much as a

66

second of my life, I wake up and leap to my feet, ready to take on another challenging day. But Ella likes to sneak up on it. She isn't really awake until after breakfast.

"But there are dozens of bed and breakfasts around here," said Ella. Sleepiness makes her argumentative. "You have no idea which one they're in."

"That's why I need you. You and your car."

"But—"

I didn't have time to stand there bickering with her. It was already nearly eight-thirty. "I'll be over as soon as I get dressed," I told her – and hung up the phone.

Ella didn't have her car. It was in Creek's garage, being serviced.

"I tried to tell you," said Ella, "but as usual you wouldn't listen. We'll have to wait till tomorrow. I'm getting it back tonight"

Tomorrow might be another day, but it could also be a day too late. "Well, we have no choice then," I decided. "We'll have to go by bike."

"In this heat?"

"Pedal fast," I advised. "It'll create a breeze."

Ella was wrong about how many bed and breakfasts there are around Dellwood. There aren't dozens; there are hundreds. Apparently anyone with a spare room sticks a sign on the front porch and waits for the city dwellers, bored with the theatre and music and elegant dining, to flood in, desperate to see a rabbit. We spent nearly three hours riding up hill and down dale, stopping at every one we found, but no one recognized Shona or Leslie from my descriptions.

The last one we had time for was the Freistucks' "Bed & Breakfast – home cooking and TV". By then we were both grimy and aching, and so wet with sweat that we looked as though we'd just tested for our Life Saver badges.

There was a man kneeling on the lawn doing something rural in the flowerbed.

I greeted him brightly. "Hi!" I said. "We were wondering if you could help us."

The man turned around. I must've looked worse than I thought because he just stared at me for a few seconds as though he couldn't quite place the language. Then he said, "Are you from one of those cults or something?"

See what I mean about Deadwood, New Jersey? It's like stepping back in time to medieval Europe. What did he think our cult's mission was, punishing ourselves for our sins by dying of heat exhaustion?

"Of course not." I smiled reassuringly. "We're looking for the proprietor."

"Mrs Freistuck's not in." He went back to his digging.

"But you live here, right?" I asked the back of his head. "Or work here?"

He turned around again. "I'm Mr Freistuck. But whatever you're selling we've already got it."

I laughed. "Oh, no ... we're not selling anything. We're – we're looking for my aunt and her friend."

Ella had been following me slowly up the driveway as though she was dragging a loaded Conastoga wagon behind her, but now I heard her stop before she reached us.

"She staying here?" asked Mr Freistuck.

"That's what I'm trying to find out." I gave a girlish laugh. "Silly me, I forgot to write down the name of the B & B she's at. But I know it's around here. Somewhere."

Mr Freistuck looked yearningly at the spade in his hand and sighed. "What's your aunt's name?"

I told him her name.

Mr Freistuck shook his head. "First names don't mean nothing to me. What's her last name?"

It was hard not to let my smile lapse. None of the other people we'd asked had been as difficult as to ask for a surname. I put this down to the fact that Mr Freistuck wasn't a woman like the others – and also to the fact that he obviously enjoyed digging in the dirt. I find that people like Karen Kapok, who get pleasure from soil, have a tendency to be niggly and pedantic.

"Well..." I glanced behind to Ella for moral support and possibly help, but she had her back to me and was staring out at the road. "Well, it sort of depends."

Mr Freistuck absentmindedly stabbed at the earth a few times. "Depends on what?"

"She's from the city," I explained. "You know what city people are like. It depends on her mood. Sometimes she uses her maiden name, sometimes she uses her married name, sometimes she uses—"

"What kind of car does she drive?"

"Car?"

Mr Freistuck had hidden depths of sarcasm you wouldn't expect from someone wearing a Hal's Hardware baseball cap. "You need me to explain what a car is?"

"No, of course not. It's just that – it's just that she's just got a new one and I'm not sure—"

"Do you know what she looks like?" asked Mr Freistuck. "Or has she had plastic surgery since the last time you saw her?"

I described Shona. "She's about five-foot seven, has three studs in her right ear, short black hair, a slightly long nose, wears Chanel No. 5, and looks like she might be Armenian or possibly Welsh and probably likes Miles Davis."

Not so much a flicker of recognition showed in Mr Freistuck's eyes, but I didn't take this as a no. He seemed to me like the kind of man who might not recognize a detailed description of his wife.

"Her friend's name is Leslie." I described Leslie.

"She doesn't have a last name either?"

"Oh of course she does." I smiled staunchly. "But I don't remember what it is."

Mr Freistuck hefted his spade. "Yeah, I know who you mean."

"Oh, but that's terrific!" Even though Mr

Freistuck was clearly an undemonstrative man, I wanted to hug him. "Where are they? Are they here?"

He turned again and resumed his digging. "Nope."

"Well do you mind if we wait?" Ella had her cell phone. I figured I could call Mrs Magnolia and tell her I was going to be late.

"You can do what you like, just let me get on with my work in peace."

Full of jubilation, I started back towards Ella when, from deep in the border, Mr Freistuck said, "Course, they're not staying here any more."

I turned sharply. "What?"

"Moved out," said Mr Freistuck. "Somebody gave them a house."

My heart was lower than the bottom of a well and just as dark as I finally made my way to the store. There was no doubt in my mind that my only contacts with the production crew were now living in Carla Santini's back yard. They might as well be in Peru, for all the good that did me.

But coincidence is not just the stuff of fiction; it's the stuff of life as well. I was just gliding to a stop in front of Second Best when I saw Shona and Leslie coming out of a store across the street. Pushing my bike, I raced across the road.

"Hi!" I called, not quite managing to stop before I hit their rear bumper with my front tyre. "Remember me?"

They both looked up, smiling vaguely, their hands on the doors of their car. As difficult as it is to believe, they didn't remember me. I put this down to the pressures of work.

"I'm sorry," Leslie began, "I don't think…"

"The other day," I prompted. "In the second-hand clothes store?"

Shona kept looking at me as if she was flicking through her memory files without coming up with a match, but Leslie nodded slowly. "Oh yeah, that's right. You sold us a bowling shirt."

Shona got into the driver's seat. "Nice to see you again." She slammed the door shut.

Like an echo, Leslie's door shut right after it.

I stretched over the handlebars and tapped on Shona's window. "Please!" I shouted. "I just – I wanted to ask you a question."

There was a whirring sound and the window lowered halfway. It just proves how phony Hollywood people really are. Both of them had been all smiles and pleasantries when they came to the store but now, although they were technically smiling, they looked about as pleasant as the gout.

"What is it?" asked Shona. She started the engine.

I said I remembered they said the movie needed extras and I was just wondering if there was some way I could be one without having to stand in a line with everyone else. "You know," I said, "I am an actor myself. I—"

She cut me off before I could give her my

résumé. "I'm afraid we work in costume, not casting."

I had to speak quickly because the window was rising again. "Oh, I know ... I just thought – because you said—"

She beeped the horn so I could get out of the way before she backed over me.

I threw myself into work that afternoon so I wouldn't become negative after the horrendous start to my day. I sorted through the new consignment; I changed the price tags on things that had been on the racks so long they seemed as permanent as the door; I bubbled with efficiency and helpfulness and hummed cheerful songs under my breath.

"Well, you certainly seem to be in a good mood today," commented Mrs Magnolia.

I believe in total honesty whenever possible. "I'm not," I said. "I'm just trying to keep up my spirits."

"That's my girl," said Mrs Magnolia.

I shouldn't've bothered. Although it's not true of water, food, money, rainforests or clean air, it is true that there's no limit to the defeats and humiliations a person can suffer in this world.

I was rereading *Othello* during a shopping lull to take my mind off my own problems (nobody does problems like the Bard – not even me) when I heard the door open, and looked up to see Carla Santini and Alma Vitters. Carla's often said that diamonds are the only things she would ever wear secondhand, but from the way she strode into the store you'd think the sign outside said Prada.

She feigned surprise at seeing me behind the counter.

"Oh my God, Lola! I totally forgot you work here." Of course she had. "I just had to get out of the house for a while. I mean, you wouldn't believe what it's like! They're starting the shoot in a couple of days, so we've already got Bret and Lucy in the guestrooms and the costume designers and wardrobe people in the cottage because they need so much space. It's total chaos – I feel like I'm living in a boarding house. Not that they aren't all really sweet. Especially Lucy. She's just as nice as she can be. Being a big star hasn't spoiled her at all."

So that was why she'd dropped by: to rub it in. "I guess we all have our crosses to bear," I murmured.

"Don't we just?" laughed Carla. "So we found ourselves passing by and I thought, hey why not go in?" It was like the Queen stopping her carriage because she'd never been in that McDonald's on the corner. "Daddy's sure our maid sells some of the stuff my mother gives her to Mrs Magnolia." Then, in case I'd leapt to the wrong conclusion, added, "Not that he's ever come in here of course."

Alma rolled her eyes. "Well, why would he?"

"So you know, I thought, why don't I just have a look? It isn't right if she is selling Mommy's gifts to her, is it?" Carla's smile was serene.

I smiled back. "Maybe if you paid her a living wage she wouldn't have to."

"I really am going to miss your New York sense of humour." She gave a small and painful laugh to prove it. "It's so refreshing."

I spread my arms wide to include every corner of the room. "So now that you're here, what do you think? See anything you recognize?"

Alma snorted, which I took as a no. "You know..." Alma's voice slithered around us. "I always thought old clothes all went to Christian Aid charities and stuff like that. You know, for really poor people in the Third World." She looked around. "This place is really..." She searched her vocabulary (usually limited to the names of designers and "Yes, Carla" and "Oh, Carla") for a word that might describe a store that sold nothing that was outrageously expensive or new. "Different."

Carla cocked her pretty head to one side. "It's got a really down-home feel, hasn't it? You just know ordinary people shop here." The floodlight of her smile fell on me. And worked here, too, obviously.

I picked up my book again. "Shucks," I said in a real down-home twang. "You just holler if you need any help."

Things Are Bad, Then Things Get Worse

I had a date with Sam that night. I wasn't really in the mood (there's nothing like an encounter with Carla Santini to demolish a person's *joie de vivre*), but a great actor has to be able to rise above her moods. You have to put on your costume and make-up and get out on that stage no matter what state your personal life is in. Your heart may be in more pieces than a broken windshield, but if the evening's fare is a comedy, you still have to make the audience smile and laugh and forget their woes. So I put myself in a cheerful, positive frame of mind and resolved to forget about the movie for at least one night.

Sam picked me up after work in his dad's van (you can barely fit people in his Karmann Ghia, never mind a bicycle).

We went to Triolo's for pizza (even though it's miles out of town in the middle of nowhere) because Sam fixes Mr Triolo's car and Mr Triolo loves him. We always get a salad or dessert on the house.

"Well if you ask me it's pretty astonishingly ironic that I'm the one who heard about the movie first and Carla's the one who gets to be in it," I was saying as we reached Triolo's.

"Twenty." Sam sighed. "That's the twentieth time you've mentioned either the movie or the Santini since we left the store." He pulled into a space near the entrance. "I don't know what you're so het up about. I thought the Cep-Santini War was over. I thought you had nothing but contempt for Tinsel Town."

It's astounding how photographic everyone's memory is when it comes to something I said.

"I'm not het up," I informed him indignantly. "All I said was that I think it's grossly unfair that Carla not only gets everything she wants, but things she doesn't want too. And that I should've known better than to try to get anywhere asking minions. It's like asking the prop person to tell you how to interpret your lines."

Sam turned off the ignition and looked at me. "OK, you're not het up — but since you've just spent the whole ride over talking about Carla and this dumb movie, do you think we could have a moratorium on all conversation involving them — at least till after we've eaten?"

I said, "Of course." It's not like I've got an obsessive personality.

Most of the light in Triolo's comes from candles

stuck in wine bottles, which makes it very atmospheric, but pretty dark too. We sat at the front near the window so we could see what we were eating.

It'd be as hard to have a bad time with Sam as it would be to climb Everest with towels on your feet, so it was easy enough to stick with the moratorium. In fact, for over an hour I forgot that things like Carla Santini and Hollywood movies existed. When we were ready for dessert, Mr Triolo himself came to take our order. It's another sad fact of life that everyone has an ulterior motive, and pizza men are no exception. Mr Triolo came himself not just because he likes us, but because he wanted to know what Sam thought the new noise in his car might be. Much as I love Sam, I can't say that I share his passion for the inner workings of the automobile. So while they were discussing all the things that might make Mr Triolo's car sound as though it was about to implode, I let my eyes wander round the room. The walls are decorated with old photographs of generations of Triolos (Mr Triolo's parents on their wedding day; Mr Triolo as a child in front of an ancient hovel in the Old Country; Mr Triolo's grandfather standing in a field with a dog).

I was thinking that the reason Mr Triolo's pizza was so good was obviously because he came from solid peasant stock and marinara sauce flowed through his veins with the blood, when Mr Triolo must've noticed I was going into a trance and suddenly said, "Hey, Lola. You'll be interested in this. Guess who that is at the back table?"

My gaze fell on the table tucked into a dark corner at the rear of the restaurant (any further and it would've been outside). There was a couple sitting at it. He had his back to me and she was wearing a floppy hat, so it was hard to see her face. They were leaning towards each other, talking intensely. From what I could see of her mouth they were probably arguing.

I shrugged. "I give up. Who is it?"

"Oh go on…" It just shows how adding a little excitement to the most prosaic lives (by filming a movie in their town, for instance) can change people. Mr Triolo's always been a man I associate with flour and cheese, and not with a carefree, exuberant nature, but now he gave me a playful poke with the menu. "I'll give you a hint. The guy's producing that movie they're making here."

Sam groaned out loud. "For Chrissake, Sal. Not you, too."

Mr Triolo and I both ignored him.

"Really? Hal Minsky?" I'd read his name in the local paper. Nonetheless, I wasn't sure Mr Triolo could be trusted on matters of Hollywood trivia. He once boasted that he hadn't gone to a movie since John Wayne died. "Are you sure?"

Mr Triolo nodded. "Waitress heard them talking when she brought them their drinks. That's when she recognized the young lady."

I squinted into the gloom at the rear of the

restaurant. I could make out a few golden locks peeking out from the woman's hat. But it was the mouth that gave her away. The collagen injections made it look infected.

Because of Sam's lousy attitude about the movie and everything connected to it, I hid my excitement. "Why that's Lucy Rio, isn't it?" I made it sound like I was identifying a pizza by its ingredients; mozzarella *and* goat's cheese with capers, why that must be the house special.

"Thatta girl." Mr Triolo gave me a playful wink. "Got it in one. I knew you'd know." He tapped his chest. "Me? I wouldn't know who she was unless she was wearing a nametag."

Having woken me up, Mr Triolo returned to discussing his car with Sam. I waited until they were deep in the world of spark plugs and pistons and then, very casually, I excused myself to go the ladies' room. The door that leads to the ladies' room is opposite the corner where Lucy Rio and the producer were sitting.

I walked slowly and calmly, a girl with nothing on her mind but checking that her mascara hadn't gone spiky. When I got close to their table, I stopped to look at one of the pictures on the wall (Mrs Triolo with Goofy at Disney World).

"For the last time, Lucy, it's impossible," Hal Minsky was saying. "There isn't enough room at the Santinis' for another fifty people. You'll have to live without the astrologer, the herbalist, the psychic and the aromatherapist for a few weeks."

So much for Lucy Rio not being spoiled by being a big star.

"I don't see why we can't go to a hotel," said Lucy Rio.

"And have the press camped outside for the duration? Have you forgotten what a bad mood having the press camped outside puts you in?"

"Not as bad a mood as living under the same roof as that jerk Bret Fork," she snapped back.

And so much for the rumour that Lucy Rio and Bret Fork were secretly dating.

"You won't say that if they get hold of that story about your father."

Lucy sniffled and her voice quivered. "That's my father's problem, not mine. I'm just an innocent victim."

Hal Minsky sighed. "And that's another thing. Enough of the fights and tantrums. You haven't been there forty-eight hours yet and already you're—"

Obviously, not as nice as she could be.

Suddenly aware of my presence, Hal Minsky glanced over at me. Acting as though I didn't even know they were there, I gave Goofy and Mrs Triolo one last affectionate smile and casually stepped through the door marked Toilets.

I locked myself in the far cubicle so I wouldn't be disturbed while I rehearsed what I was going to say. I didn't want to be too obvious (Lucy Rio once threw a bag of poo at a photographer for trying to take a picture of her scooping up after her dog), so

I'd pretend that it was Hal Minsky I recognized. "Excuse me," I'd say. "I don't want to bother you, but don't I know you from somewhere? You seem really familiar. Do you work around here?" Then, to throw him off his guard, I'd say, "Maybe in the Walmart? Or at the gas station?" Then – suddenly and with an endearing touch of embarrassment – I'd recognize him. "Oh, I don't believe it," I'd gasp. "You don't work in Walmart. I know who you are. You're Hal Minsky, the famous producer, aren't you?" Everybody knows how egocentric movie people are, so I figured the famous bit would make him mellow and allow me to go on. I'd tell him how, as an aspiring actor myself, I'd always admired his work. "Oh, of course," I'd say. "How *could* I forget? Carla Santini did say you were in town." He'd be delighted to discover I was a friend of Carla's. He'd say, "You know, we are looking for a few extras, if you wanted to come along…" I'd be surprised – happily, but modestly, surprised.

After I finished my rehearsal, I had to touch up my make-up and make adjustments to my hair of course. First impressions are very important. There was some old movie star Mrs Baggoli once told us about who was discovered sitting at the counter in a soda fountain. Think of it. If she'd been having a really bad hair day, or had a spot on the end of her nose like a Christmas light, she would never have been noticed. She would've ended up going back to the boring little town she came from, her dreams all turned to dust, and ended up

82

overweight and working in a diner.

When I was finally ready I stood behind the door for a few seconds, controlling my breathing. Then I counted to three, pushed open the door and stepped through.

Hal Minsky and Lucy Rio were on their feet. She was standing at his shoulder, still talking at him and swinging her bag as if she might hit him with it. He was concentrating on taking his receipt from the little plastic tray. They were ready to leave.

It's true that under our veneer of civilization the primitive man still lives. In that instant, the same instincts that guided my ancestors when confronted with angry woolly mammoths took over. Spurred on not by thought but by the need to survive, I flung myself across the space that separated them from me.

"Mr Minsky!" I cried. "Mr Minsky, if you could just wait one minute, I really have to talk to you."

He didn't even look at me. "I'm afraid you've made a mistake." He took Lucy Rio's arm and yanked her towards the door. She stepped on my foot.

But a little pain wouldn't have deterred my ancestors and it didn't deter me. I grabbed hold of his elbow. "No, I haven't made a mistake. I know you're Hal Minsky. I've seen your picture in the paper. I—"

He finally looked at me. Well, he looked at the hand that was holding onto him. "Would you mind letting go of my arm?"

"But I really have to talk to you."

"I'm not going to ask you politely again."

I let go. "I'm sorry, Mr Minsky, I'm really sorry, but it's extremely important that I—"

"I'm warning you young lady, if you don't leave me alone I'm calling the manager."

Young lady? I always imagined movie people were really hip and cool, but he sounded astoundingly like my mother. I was so surprised I took a step backwards. "But I—"

"I don't know who this person is you're confusing me with, but for that last time – I am not he."

"But Mr Minsky, I'm a friend of Carla Santini's."

This announcement had the same effect on him that it would have had on me. He gave Lucy Rio a shove that made her stagger. "Damn hick towns. Come on, let's get out of here." He bolted for the exit.

I think my jaw fell open. *Damn hick towns?* Was he calling *me* a hick?

I watched them steam to the front and out of the door. I was too numb with shock to even think of going after them.

"You know, I did recognize him," said Sam when I got back to our table. "I saw him being interviewed once. He's that dude who made that crappy movie about the President getting abducted by aliens. What'd you say his name is?"

I eyed him coldly. Talk about going back to your boring little town with your dreams all turned to dust. "I'm sorry," I said, "but I promised I wouldn't talk about the movie tonight."

My mother was in the living room reading a book when I got home. She glanced over as I hurtled into the room.

"Have a nice time, Mary?"

Despite my disappointment at the way Hal Minsky had treated me I was in a good mood. I'd got close. It was a sign from the gods of theatre that the next time I'd be successful.

"I had a great time." I threw myself into the nearest chair. "Wait'll you hear what happened. You won't believe it. Lucy Rio was in the restaurant! Isn't that incredible? She was practically at the next table."

"Who?" asked my mother.

[Cue: look of endless suffering at the hands of philistines.] "Lucy Rio? The actor?"

Karen Kapok yawned. "Never heard of her."

"Of course you've heard of her. She's the one who was in—"

But I didn't get a chance to tell her what movies Lucy Rio'd been in because at that moment my sisters charged into the room shrieking as if there were tigers after them.

"Calm down," I ordered. "I can't understand what you're saying. Tell me slowly – and one at a time."

They didn't of course. They both shouted at once. "Guess what, Mary? Guess what, Mary? We're going to be in a movie!"

This time I heard exactly what they said. I gazed at them as Lot must have gazed at the pillar of salt that had been his wife. Of what cruel ironies is life composed! Of what sad truths! The only talent either of my sisters has ever shown is for cheating at Monopoly, and the one time we took them to a real play (without singing and dancing) they both fell asleep. And here they were about to appear in *my* Hollywood film.

"*You're* going to be in the movie? Are you sure you're not deluding yourselves? I don't know who told you that, but they could be wrong. You know what this hick town is like for rumours." Like warm, moist lungs to a viral infection.

"But it's true! Oona May at day camp said so." Karen Kapok was nodding.

I gave Pam and Paula a concerned, sisterly smile. "But you can't act."

"They don't have to act," said my mother. "All they have to do is sit."

Apparently they were using all the kids in the day camp for a scene that called for a school bus full of children.

"Aren't you happy for us?" asked Paula.

"Don't you think it's cool?" asked Pam.

"Of course I'm happy for you." But how could my soul not wince at the bitter twists of Fate? "Of course I think it's cool." But how could my heart not sigh at the sad reality of a world where chance beats the stuffing out of genius? What with one thing and another I'd had a very frustrating and stressful day. I didn't really want to spend the rest of it listening to them yammering on about their one-and-a-half seconds of fame. I clutched my forehead. "Unfortunately, I'm not really feeling too well. I'm going to bed. I think I'm getting a migraine."

"You don't get migraines," said my mother.

I closed my eyes against the pain. "I do now."

Giving Up Is Not In My Nature

In my experience (which is considerable considering my youth), spiritual exhaustion is just as debilitating as physical exhaustion, and my spirit was as limp as a rag. I couldn't face going to work the next morning. My heart was scarred by the cruel twists of fate it had suffered and my soul was passed out cold. I rang Mrs Magnolia and told her that the washing machine had gone berserk and I had to help my mother so I'd be in late.

I stayed in bed, listening to my favourite CD and thinking spiritually nourishing thoughts. Time does really heal and music does really soothe the ravaged soul. After only a couple of hours my resilient nature rose up like a phoenix from the ashes of despair. (Being me is a little like being a mail person. You know, neither rain, nor snow, nor dark of night shall stop this courier from completing her appointed rounds – and neither surly costume designers, nor irritable producer, nor Carla Santini will make me give up.) After all, I realized, it is the most ordinary people who are often the most lucky. And I don't think it's something you can really begrudge them. It's the gods' way of balancing things out. You know, because these people aren't gifted, their souls are as flightless as the dodo and their hearts are nourished on the spiritual equivalent of potato chips and diet soda, the gods let them win the lottery. What else do they have to look forward to, poor things? But those of us who are gifted, who have soaring souls and hearts that are nourished by the spiritual equivalent of lentil stew and greens, don't have to rely on luck. We make our own.

By the time I got to work I was in my usual upbeat mood.

"Everything all right?" asked Mrs Magnolia as I came whistling into the store.

"Red alert over," I cried. "The flood's been staunched and all is well."

"Thank heaven for that," said Mrs Magnolia. "When mine overflowed we had to rip the whole floor up."

"Gosh..." I shook my head in sympathy.

Mrs Magnolia smiled sadly over the rack she was hanging blouses on. I thought she was still thinking about her floor. "What a shame that you weren't here this morning, though. You'll never guess who came in."

With hindsight I can see that a three-year-old with ADD would have been able to guess who it was, so surely I should have, but I was in such a positive, who-needs-luck kind of mood that I didn't. I said, "The First Lady?" Like Carla Santini, she likes to keep in touch with the poor.

Mrs Magnolia giggled, which I have to say I don't find attractive in anyone over ten, never mind forty. "Oh, no, no, no one like that. No one really important." Hangers jangled as Mrs Magnolia hooked them onto the rack.

Personally, although I'm sure the First Lady's a very nice woman, I don't count her as really important. Mostly what she does is stand next to her husband, holding the dog and smiling.

"Mrs Carlucci?" I wheeled my bike to the back. Mrs Carlucci used to be one of our best customers, but she hadn't been in since she bought a chenille robe that brought her out in a rash and blamed Mrs Magnolia, so I figured maybe she'd finally called a truce.

It wasn't Mrs Carlucci.

"A very nice man who's shooting a movie around here."

I was in the storeroom when Mrs Magnolia uttered these words, but I came out faster than you can say "Cut!"

"What?"

"I think he said he was the director." She held up a floral blouse, eyeing it dubiously. "Or was it the producer?" She shrugged in the way of a woman who is used to customers returning things. "One of those."

90

A golden ray of hope rose up to warm my soul. Maybe the costume designers had told Charley Hottle about me after all. You know: *Don't we need someone to be waiting at the stop for the school bus? Well, there's this terrific girl who works in the secondhand store who'd be perfect.*

"What was his name? Was it Hottle?"

Mrs Magnolia blinked. "He didn't say."

"Well what did he want?" I was as casual as a T-shirt and a pair of jeans.

Mrs Magnolia slipped the floral blouse into the clump of patterned blouses. "Oh ... just to chat about the town, find out where things are, that kind of thing. It seems they'll be here for several weeks."

"Really?" My heart was pounding away like a flamenco dancer. What other crucial pieces of information had Mrs Magnolia gleaned in her conversation with maybe the director or maybe the producer? I opened my eyes wide as though this was all news to me. "Geez... I wonder where they'll stay."

"Oh, I really don't know. Not now the hotel's closed down." The Dellwood Hotel closed down due to lack of interest in the sixties and was finally converted into apartments in the eighties. She shrugged. "I suppose there are quite a few bed and breakfasts around."

And I had the aching muscles to prove that I'd been to most of them.

I took up my position behind the counter.

"Yeah, I suppose there are."

It may have been the shocking-pink blouse she was holding now, but it almost looked as though Mrs Magnolia was blushing. "But guess what else?"

The way Fate was fighting against me I was almost afraid to. "He gave you a part?"

"Oh no. I wouldn't want to be in a movie. It's so public." Unlike running a store. "It's Betsy."

"Excuse me?"

"Betsy," repeated Mrs Magnolia. "You know. My husband's car." Mr Magnolia owns a 1956 baby-blue Chevy that he's always fussing over. I once leaned on it really lightly and he acted as if I'd whacked it with an axe. "Mr Santini told him about it."

Was everyone and everything going to get a part except me? I smiled as though this was exactly what I'd been hoping to hear. "Wasn't that nice of him," I said.

As soon as my mother and her other daughters retreated to the living room to be mindlessly entertained by the TV after supper I got out the local phone book and called every hotel that was listed. I used an English accent, which I'm good at since I was raised on the Public Broadcasting Service. (I read somewhere that Americans respond well to English accents. They think they sound educated and trustworthy.)

"Pardon me for troubling you," I said, "but I

92

understand a friend of mine is staying with you ...
Hottle ... Charles Hottle..." Maybe he was using
a different name. "Are you certain?" I persisted.
"He's from Hollywood. He's making a film."

I know I wasn't born to be a loser – to live an
unsung, mediocre existence and then die in some
nursing home with drool down the corner of my
mouth – but sometimes even I start to wonder. The
only positive response I got was at the last hotel in
the book, but that wasn't because the film crew
was staying there. It was because the desk clerk
came from Manchester. He was so excited you'd
think I was his long-lost sister. "Where are you
from?" he demanded. I couldn't very well say from
a production of *Emma* so I hung up.

Paula came into the kitchen as I put down the
receiver.

"Who are you calling?" Her eyes were on the
phone book.

"No one you know."

Paula's spirit is not artistic, but she is observant
and her eyesight's perfect. "Why were you calling
hotels? Are you and Sam going to have sex?"

I slammed the phone book shut. "No, Sam and
I are not going to have sex. But you'll be the first
to know if we do."

She opened the fridge and took out the jug of
iced tea. "So why were you calling hotels? Were
you trying to find the movie people?"

And although not blessed with any signs of
brilliance, Paula does have a logical mind.

"And why would I want to do that?" I stuffed the book back into its home in the old school desk Karen Kapok uses as a phone table. "You know I have no interest in the tawdry glitter and tinsel that is Hollywood. My heart and soul belong to the theatre where the pain and joy of human life are given substance and flesh – not to the shadow puppet show of the celluloid world."

"Oh." She started filling three glasses with the tea. "Because Oona May says they're starting to film on Friday and she knows where."

I stared at the back of my sister's head. "Oona May?"

Paula finished pouring iced tea all over the counter and returned the jug to the fridge. "Yeah, you know, because she's in charge of the day camp so she knows stuff like that. You know, because we're going to be in the movie."

I ask you: how ironic is life? Oona May Paduski was in radio communication with planet Hollywood while I was lost in space.

"Really?" I went over to help her put the glasses on a tray. "So where are they shooting?"

"Why?" Paula slid the tray from the counter. "I thought you didn't care."

"I don't care. But Ella would like to know." The twins really like Ella. They think she's normal.

"She would?" Paula eyed me silently for a few seconds. She looked just like Karen Kapok, only much shorter and there wasn't any clay in her hair. "What's it worth?"

*   *   *

The first day of shooting was taking place outside of town, at this dilapidated old house on Bluff Road. Because it was imperative that I be there, I called Mrs Magnolia as soon as my alarm went off that morning.

"I'm so sorry, Mrs Magnolia," I fairly sobbed into the phone, "but I can't come in today. I've got the most awful headache."

"Lola?" Mrs Magnolia is obviously a slow riser like Ella.

"I wanted to be sure I got you before you left for the store."

"Lola, do you know what time it is?"

It was seven. I needed at least an hour to get dressed for what I hoped was the first day of my Hollywood career. Of course I had to bend the truth just a little for Mrs Magnolia. "Not really..." My voice was soft and tight with pain. "I can hardly see. I think I must have a migraine, Mrs Magnolia. It feels like someone's turning screws in my brain."

As my mother pointed out, I don't actually get migraines, but Mrs Magnolia does so I knew she'd be sympathetic.

"Oh, you poor thing..." Her voice sounded as if it was wincing in empathy. "Of course you can't come in if you feel like that. Have you thrown up yet? You should feel better once you throw up."

I thanked her for being so understanding.

It took me nearly the hour I'd allotted just to

decide what I was wearing. I needed both to stand out from the good but hopelessly ordinary people of Dellwood – and look just like them at the same time. Fortunately, great actors enjoy a challenge, and I am no exception. In the end I chose a short, cotton, floral skirt that subtly evoked the exotic island of Hawaii, four-inch wedge sandals to subtly suggest I stood above the rest, and the Creek's Auto Repairs promotional T-shirt Sam gave me for Christmas (he hates shopping) to subtly suggest that though tall and exotic I was very much a part of the town. Then I fastened my hair all over my head with brightly coloured butterfly clips for the final touch of funky sophistication that would let them know I wasn't a hick.

For once I hadn't had to use all my considerable powers of persuasion to get Ella to agree to go with me.

"Sure," said Ella. "It'll be more fun than lying around the pool all day." How some of us have to suffer.

From half a mile away we saw the cars parked along the road up ahead and a really large crowd of people just standing around. If we didn't know they were filming a movie we would've thought something awful had happened.

"Maybe this wasn't such a good idea after all," said Ella. "I've never seen this many people together even on the last night of the Fireman's Fair."

"Well this *is* more interesting than a ferris wheel that's always breaking down and corn on the cob." But I was surprised too. All these people couldn't be from Dellwood, or even be friends of Carla's. There were hundreds of them. Where on earth had they come from? Didn't any of them have jobs or families to look after?

We decided to leave the car where it was so it wouldn't take hours to get back out again, and walked the rest of the way until we reached the rear of the teeming throng.

Ella, daughter of a woman who believes dirt and germs to be her personal enemies, held herself stiffly and awkwardly, trying to avoid having her face pressed into some stranger's sweaty back. "I told you this wasn't a good idea. We can't move and we can't see what's going on."

This was true. The only movement was a restless, side-to-side shuffle, and even on four-inch heels I couldn't see anything but baseball caps.

"Don't worry. Something will happen soon," I assured her.

This proved to be optimistic. Minutes passed, and then tens of minutes, but the only thing that happened was that we started sweating pretty markedly. So much for the glamour and excitement of Hollywood.

"I'd rather be stuck in a traffic jam. At least you can listen to the radio," whispered Ella. "And anyway, it's pointless. There must be a thousand people ahead of us. We don't have a chance of

97

getting a walk-on."

It was time to take some action. I tapped the man in front of me on the shoulder. "Excuse me, sir, but do you know what's going on up there?"

He didn't know.

I tried the woman next to him. "Is anything happening?" I asked.

She wanted to know how she should know.

I sidled past a few people, dragging Ella with me and getting some really dirty looks. Like warrior kings, no one was prepared to give up any ground.

"Are they taking on extras?" I asked the backs of heads. "Is this the line?"

A woman (who if you ask me was really much too old to be standing around in the heat like that, especially without a hat) suggested that I find out for myself.

Did I look like I was from *Starship Enterprise* and could be beamed around at will? Because that was the only way we could've gone more than an inch or two without inciting a riot. We might as well have been standing behind a brick wall.

"Well," sighed Ella, "I guess we'll just have to wait with everybody else and hope for the best."

But I'm not everybody else. I have to admit that I was disappointed in Ella. After all we'd been through together she'd forgotten one of Life's greatest lessons.

Ella caught my look. "What?"

"The mouse waits," I reminded her. "But the eagle acts."

98

"The eagle can fly," snapped Ella. "It makes it easier to get through crowds."

"We don't have to go through." I started moving towards the side of the road. "We can go around."

"Around?" Ella looked at the hilly woods that run along the beach road on either side. "You mean go through *there*? In skirts and sandals?"

"Of course not. I don't want to end up with poison ivy and leaves in my hair. I mean go back to the car and take the other road to the beach. Then we can walk along the shore and get to the shoot from the other end."

Instead of greeting this plan with the enthusiasm it deserved, Ella squinched her face up in the way she does when she thinks I'm about to go too far, and said, "Oh, Lola... I don't know..."

"What do you mean you 'don't know'? I thought you were tired of sunning yourself by the pool. I thought you wanted to have some fun." I touched her arm, gently but pleadingly. "Come on, let's get the car."

There was a small public beach about a mile away that Karen Kapok took us to once when we first moved to Deadwood so we could bask in some of the benefits of not living in New York City. (Paula got sunburnt, Pam wouldn't go in the water because she was convinced it was toxic and someone else's psychotic child smashed his ice pop on my head.)

The public beach was even smaller than I

99

remembered. (Which isn't hard to understand since I had largely blocked the whole ugly afternoon from my mind.) It consisted of about three yards of boardwalk, several square yards of sand, a small brick building that contained toilets and a snack bar, and a lifeguard stand (but no lifeguard). There was a jetty of boulders separating the beach from the coast running north under the cliffs.

Ella stared up the coast as if she was hoping to see some friendly Indians paddling towards us with help and advice. "It seems to go on for ever." She sounded nervous.

"It's a shoreline, not the universe. And anyway the house can't be that far along."

"I have a question," said Ella.

"Now what?"

"How will we know when we're there? It all looks the same."

"We'll see the house, won't we? I know what it looks like." I had a vague memory. "We've driven by it lots of times." That one time, when we got lost on our way to this beach.

Ella turned her eyes to the cliffs. "And how do we get up there?"

"There'll be stairs of course." It stood to reason; there had to be. "You don't build a house by the beach if you can't get down to it, do you?" I certainly hoped not.

It wasn't until we'd crossed the jetty that another reason why no one else had thought of

100

coming at the film crew this way occurred to me.

"What happened to the sand?" demanded Ella.

I stared down. The sand had vanished beneath several inches of ocean that was carpeted with rocks. From what I could make out through the rippling water and clots of seaweed, these rocks had yet to be smoothed and rounded by erosion.

"How would I know? I'm an actor not a geologist." I kicked off my shoes.

"We can't walk on those stones in bare feet," Ella protested. "If we don't bleed to death, we'll get some major infection."

"I'll take my chances." I stuck my shoes in my bag. "I can't walk through that water in shoes." Thank God my skirt was so short.

"But it's filthy." Ella's nose wrinkled in distaste. She's definitely going to look like her mother when she gets older.

"It could be worse," I said. "It could be burning like the Cuyahoga River used to."

"Well lucky us," muttered Ella.

It was slow going. Beneath the murky surface the rocks were slick with primal slime and the sand was mined with objects even sharper than the stones. The tourist brochures urge you to enjoy a day of fun and sun at the Jersey shore, but, personally, I'd rather be watching debris drift by on the East River – and from the way Ella kept whimpering I guessed she'd agree. We made our way – tiny step by tiny step – slipping, splashing and bleeding from multiple wounds.

I examined my left foot with a certain amount of concern. "I didn't know God armed the ocean," I muttered.

"I don't think God did." Ella fished a piece of rusted can from the water and held it up. "I don't think God drinks Bud."

We trudged on. A great actor has to trust herself unconditionally of course or she'd never have her first audition, but the further we went the more tiny doubts buzzed around me like sand flies. What if we were going in the wrong direction after all? What if there weren't any stairs and we had to climb up the cliff face? I gazed at the craggy rocks. We weren't really dressed for mountaineering. If I'd been alone I might have given up, but, for all her wonderful qualities, Ella does have a tendency to remind you that she told you not to do something when it turns out she was right, so there was no way I was giving in until I absolutely had to (like I was about to bleed to death). And then, as I was swatting away a few more flies, I finally saw part A of the goal of our quest, clinging to the cliffs like a vine.

"There!" I cried jubiliantly, pointing skyward. "I see the stairs!"

Ella was in her Cassandra mode. "That's the famous staircase?" She sounded dubious. "But they don't come all the way down."

This was true. Years of disuse had taken their toll and the last length of steps had fallen away and lay in a heap on the ground. I considered this a minor detail.

"They come down most of the way. We just have to climb a little to reach them."

"Are you nuts? By the time we get up there, the only movie we'll get a part in is one where some creature crawls out of a swamp." I opened my mouth to answer this argument, but Ella answered it for me. "I know, I know..." she sighed. "You haven't come this far to give up now."

You can't get away from it: chance plays a really big part in life. Think how different things would be if Columbus had taken the usual route to India. Or if the natives of the Americas had slaughtered the white men instead of helping them out. Or if nobody had been slaughtered. If the white men had said, "Hey, that's cool. You live your way and we'll go back to Europe and live our way." If the South had won the Civil War. If Jesus had been a girl. None of those things happened, of course.

And Ella and I didn't reach the film crew at the very moment that they were desperately looking around for two teenage girls with bleeding feet, wet clothes and sand and beach grass in their hair, either.

Gasping for air, we staggered around the side of the house at the exact and precise moment that Lucy Rio's character was giving this big speech to her mother about how much she didn't want to be there. Which meant that our arrival on the set didn't have quite the effect I'd hoped for.

Someone screamed, "Cut!"

103

And Charley Hottle bellowed, "What the hell are those girls doing on the set?"

Lucy Rio burst into tears and ran for her trailer.

The actor who was playing her mother said, "Great. Here we go again!"

That was the cue for everyone else to start yelling.

Charley Hottle groaned and threw the script he was holding onto an empty chair. "I'm getting a coffee unless somebody's got a bottle of hooch stashed away somewhere."

Someone yelled, "All right, everybody! Take five!"

Holding myself with as much dignity as someone who looks like she's been shipwrecked can, I grabbed hold of Ella and marched after Charley Hottle.

"Mr Hottle!" I called. "If you'll just give me a second to ex—"

My words were cut short by the sudden arrival in my life of a very large man with very strong hands who took hold of me and Ella none too gently and started propelling us towards the road. "Off. No one but crew's allowed on the set."

"If you could just wait one minute. I really have to talk to Charley Hottle. It's very important. In fact, you could say it's a matter of life and death, my mother's—"

Not only was he not listening, he was moving so fast that we were almost at the security cordon.

"You don't understand!" I wailed. "I'm a friend

of Carla Santini's. She's expecting me."

If you think about it logically, there has got to
be a God. There's just no way that all the truly
incredible things that are constantly happening to
me could possibly be caused by blind luck. There
has to be someone at the controls. Someone who
likes to give me a challenge.

What happened on the movie set is an example
of what I mean.

As soon as I said "I'm a friend of Carla Santini's", Mr Muscle came to a dead stop.

"Not another one," he muttered. He looked at
the crew that hadn't abandoned the set. "Hey!
Anybody know where the Santini kid is?"

"You mean Dellwood's answer to Fellini?"
called someone.

Everyone laughed.

The cameraman shook his head. "The last time
I saw her she was taking pictures of Lucy."

"I think she was going to shoot Bret eating his
lunch," said one of the sound guys.

Mr Muscle sighed. "Can somebody please go
and find her? Tell her two more of her best friends
have shown up."

The perfect end to a truly awful day.

I glanced over at Ella, who was staring back at
me, her eyes so wide they looked like they were
going to fall out and drop to the ground.

"Oh, that's OK." I looked right at him. People
trust you more when you make eye contact.
"Really. We didn't mean to cause you any trouble.

And we definitely don't want to waste any more of your time. I'm an actor myself, so I know how valuable it—"

"Hey! Carla!" He waved over my head. "You've got visitors."

As though we were no more than crumbs of iron and there was a giant magnet behind us, Ella and I both turned around.

Carla was just stepping out of one of the trailers parked on the side of the road. She was dry, clean and unbloodied of course. Bret Fork was standing in the doorway behind her, punching numbers into his cell phone.

I figured there were several options open to us. We could dematerialize. Or Superman could suddenly swoop down and carry us off. Or we could just pass out on the spot – that kind of manoeuvre had worked for me before.

But before I could gracefully swoon and crumble, Carla caught sight of us. She didn't blink.

"Who is it?" Her smile was bright and hopeful; her curls shimmered as though ruffled by a balmy breeze. "Where are they?"

Mr Muscle patted our shoulders. "Right here."

But maybe all wasn't lost. The other option was the old double-bluff.

"Carla!" I called. "I'm sorry we're late. I know we promised but we—"

Carla's smile became puzzled. She looked straight into my eyes. "I'm sorry..." She was practically purring. "But do I know you?"

I Try And Try Yet Again

One of Karen Kapok's major reasons for dragging us into the wastelands of New Jersey was that she wanted the twins to grow up in a real community. Every time some old lady was found decomposing in her apartment because no one knew she was dead until the stench got really bad, Karen Kapok would get onto her soap box. "You see?" she'd cry. "That wouldn't happen in a small town where people look out for each other."

And though wisdom isn't my mother's strong point, she was right about that. You can't break a fingernail at eight in the morning in Deadwood without the whole place knowing by lunchtime.

"The first thing my mom said when she got home was that someone got thrown off the movie set," Ella informed me on the phone that night. She was recovering from the traumas of the day by the pool.

"Who told her?"

"Mrs Santini. She said it was some girls from out of town. My mom was surprised it wasn't you."

"Mrs Who?" Galaxies away on the other side of town, I had my feet in a basin of water. "In case you've forgotten, we don't know anyone named Santini. We had it from the dragon's mouth."

"I wish. If that were true, when people ask me what I did on my summer vacation I wouldn't have to say 'swam, rode my bike, read a few books and got publicly humiliated.'" Ella sighed. "Well, at least we can stop now."

"Stop?" I laughed at the ludicrousness of the suggestion. "Are you nuts? We can't stop now. We may have lost the battle, but we're not going to lose the war."

Ella groaned. "You're the one who's nuts. Why can't you just quit while you're ahead – you know, like before we get arrested?"

"Because I'm going to be in that movie, that's why. Come hell or high water."

"Great," said Ella. "That's just what I wanted to hear."

Unfortunately, my resolve was slightly hampered by the fact that Ella had I had been officially forbidden from going within two miles of the movie set, but this was a small obstacle to someone of my temperament and character. If I was going to find someone who could help me get even the tiniest crumb of a part, I was going to have to get really serious and exchange my usual persona of

Lola Cep, exceptional teenager, for that of Lola Cep, super sleuth. It was too hot for a trench coat and slouch hat, but internally I decided to model myself on the great Philip Marlowe and hit the mean streets of Dellwood, New Jersey, with renewed determination. Of course, I had to be seen to go to work or Karen Kapok's suspicious instincts would've been up like a thermometer in August, but this was also a minor problem.

As soon as I'd got home I'd called Mrs Magnolia. I said my migraine wasn't any better, and that even if it was gone by the morning I'd be too exhausted, fragile and drained to contemplate going into work. Mrs Magnolia said not to worry. She once had a migraine that lasted a month.

Ella was reluctant.

"I don't think I can handle more than one public humiliation a week," said Ella. "It's bad for my self-image."

"There aren't going to be any more public humiliations," I reasoned. "This is my best plan yet."

Though creative, mine is also a logical mind. I reasoned that the members of the movie company who weren't basking in the luxurious hospitality of the Santinis (and being fed by their maid) would still need to have regular meals. So all we had to do was scout the local eateries for members of the film crew.

Ella wanted to know if I ever listened to myself. "You can't possibly actually *hear* what you're saying and still think it's a good idea," said Ella. "Do you expect us to go into every diner, fast food chain, café and restaurant in the area? Do you have some magical powers you haven't told me about?"

[Cue: the sigh of the prophet who might as well be whistling "Dixie" in an empty parking lot since nobody pays any attention to her.] "We don't have to go into every single one, El. We only go into the ones that have cars with New York number plates in the parking lot." All of the vehicles on the set and Hal Minsky's and the costume designers' cars had all been rented in the city.

"Lola." Ella was calm but firm, as though reasoning with a small child. "We're still not going to finish looking before this movie is out on DVD."

"You'll see," I said. "The gods are going to smile on us."

"If they do, it's only because they're laughing," said Ella.

Ella picked me up at dawn the next morning, wearing shades and clutching a thermos of coffee. Even though she was fully dressed, she gave the impression that she was still in her pyjamas.

"Did Marilyn give you a hard time, leaving the house so early?" I asked as I got in the car.

"She's still asleep." She passed me the coffee. "I left her a note so she doesn't think I ran away from home. What about your mom?"

There are advantages to having a mother so immersed in her work that she can't worry about

110

her child every second of the day. "She's loading the kiln. By the time she realizes I've gone she'll just think I went to work."

Just to disprove the accusation (often made by Karen Kapok, among others) that I'm as practical as a bag of crisps in the desert, I'd pored over a map of Dellwood the night before to narrow down our search. I circled an area with a five-mile radius to the movie set, which I figured was about as far as anyone was likely to go for breakfast.

"We'll start in Dellwood and work our way towards the set," I directed.

I didn't think it was likely that people from Hollywood would choose weak coffee in a Styrofoam cup and something in bread (also encased in Styrofoam) for breakfast when they could have real food on a plate and real coffee in a china cup, but Ella disagreed. She said that the reason you can find a McDonald's almost anywhere in the world isn't because no one eats in places like that. She said that she didn't get up with the fruit pickers not to be thorough.

So we started with the chains that surround the town. There were New York cars in the car parks of all of them, but on closer inspection they all belonged to bickering families in crumpled clothes or tired looking men in summer suits.

"What did I say?" I said. "These are sophisticates we're dealing with here, not hicks from the sticks. Let's try Main Street." There's a diner, a soda fountain, a Starbucks and a French café on

Main Street.

Of course, since there weren't any car parks on Main Street to check first, we had to go in each one. We decided to do it in order of cosmopolitan sophistication. We went to the café first.

After the bright lights and noise of McDonald's and the others, the café looked unnaturally dark and still inside.

"Are you sure it's open?" asked Ella as we peered through the door.

I, for one, was elated. This was just the kind of place Hollywood people would go to break their morning fast. Instead of a large, lighted menu there was a blackboard. Instead of shining plastic, there were brick walls covered with old movie posters (French, of course) and small, round wooden tables. Instead of a row of smiling faces with name-tags, there was one bored girl wearing a black apron leaning against a wooden counter.

"Of course it's open." I pointed into the continental gloom. A man and woman sat at the back, talking over their espressos. They were both dressed in jeans and T-shirts and looked like they spent a lot of time outdoors. They could be gardeners; but they could also be cameramen or something like that. "There's a couple sitting by the big Truffaut poster."

"By the what?" asked Ella.

Once again I had reason to be grateful that Fate had brought me to Ella. She'd be lost without me. "Truffaut," I repeated. "He's a very important

112

French director."

Ella said, "Oh."

I said, "Come on," and opened the door. A voice that had smoked far too many cigarettes and drunk far too much red wine was singing in French. It sounded unhappy (which isn't exactly a surprise after all that booze and tobacco). "There's a good chance they're with the movie."

I led Ella to a table near the picture of François Truffaut looking intense.

The waitress was so overjoyed to have two more customers that she was on top of us before we could sit down.

Ella looked at me. We hadn't planned to buy anything until we were sure we were in the right place and needed an excuse to hang around. But the music, the décor, and the laser-like gaze of the waitress got the better of me, and I ordered two espressos.

Our coffees were still in the machine when it became obvious that the couple at the next table weren't with the movie company. They weren't gardeners either. They were on their way to the mall to buy baby furniture.

Ella looked as though she'd known they were expecting parents the whole time. "Now what do we do?" she hissed.

I said we drank our coffees and then we paid the bill.

Ella said it was just as well I'd ordered espressos; at least they're small.

I still had high hopes that the soda fountain or

Starbucks would turn up something. The soda fountain's considered a landmark in Dellwood. In Europe something has to be around for at least five hundred years before it's considered old, but in New Jersey if something lasts fifty years it's practically ancient. The soda fountain was built in 1928 according to the front of the building, and (except for the microwave behind the counter) it pretty much looked it – chrome and Formica counter with high stools, black and white linoleum floor and soda from taps. Filmmakers looking for local colour were bound to flock there. And Starbucks was generically cosmopolitan and would at least be familiar to people from LA.

I was wrong on both counts. The soda fountain was filled with men going to work and Starbucks was filled with young mothers who didn't.

That left only the Dellwood Diner.

"You never can tell," I said optimistically as Ella and I climbed the concrete steps. "The diner is an intrinsic part of American culture. It's just the kind of place that recorders of that culture would feel at home in."

But Ella's nature is more pessimistic than mine. "Right," she muttered as we stepped through the glass door. "They've probably been lining up here since dawn to get in."

"Oh ye of little faith," I whispered as I came up behind her. "What did I tell you? Just look there!"

"Where?"

"Those two guys over there in the booth."

114

Ella's eyebrows rose in a way I found pretty irritating. "And?"

"And the one in the 'Read Orwell' T-shirt is the same guy who marched us off the set."

Ella glanced over at the man in the T-shirt, then turned back to me. "Are you sure?"

"Positive." I might forget to take out the rubbish or where the exact location of East Timor is, but I would never forget someone who's man-handled me. "I remember him vividly."

But the Gerards' only child still wasn't convinced. "Well I don't remember him."

"That's because I was trying to reason with him while you went into toxic shock. Trust me. He's got a ruby ring on his right pinky and he kept pressing it into my wrist. It really hurt."

"So what if it is him? He's not going to help us, is he?" argued Ella.

"He's not going to recognize us from the other day." I assured her. "We look totally different when we're dry and not bleeding."

Ella sighed in a resigned kind of way. "So now what do we do?"

I was about to say that we sit down in the booth behind theirs when I suddenly noticed who was at the counter no more than a few feet away from them. [Cue: gasp of shock and horror.] "Sit down! Quick!" I hurled myself into the nearest seat.

"Now what?" muttered Ella. But she followed my lead and threw herself across from me.

"Don't you see him? At the counter. Right next

115

to the booth where the movie guys are sitting."

Ella gazed around my head. "There are two men at the counter."

"The one with the baseball cap."

"They're both wearing baseball caps."

"You know, maybe *you* should think of being a lawyer," I snapped. "You'd be great on cross examinations."

"Oh excuse me," Ella snapped back. "But in case you didn't notice, they both *are* wearing baseball caps."

I was grinding my teeth so hard my jaw felt like it might snap. "The one with his hat on backwards."

"What about him?"

It never ceases to amaze me how a person can be both really smart and about as bright as a nightlight at the same time. I begged the gods for patience. "What does it *say* on the baseball cap?"

"*Creek's Auto Repairs*," read Ella. And then a happy smile lit up her face. "Is that Sam's dad? I've always wanted to meet him. He's always under a car when I go to the garage."

"Well you're not meeting him today." Is it me, or is it simply astounding how the gods can give with one hand and snatch it right back with the other? I hunkered down in my seat. "I can't let him see me." Thank God I was wearing a hat and sunglasses.

Ella gazed at me in what looked a lot like bafflement. "Why not? I thought he liked you."

"That's why. I don't want him to start chatting to us. Not in the middle of Operation Hollywood."

"There's not much of an operation if we've got to hide in this booth till he leaves," said Ella.

I picked up a menu. "Just give me a few minutes to think. I'll come up with something."

Like all great actors, I'm one of those people who works well under incredible stress. By the time the waitress brought our order I was calm and cool again – I had a plan.

"Do you think we could have the bill now?" I asked as she set two cups of tea down (neither of us could drink another coffee without risking cardiac implosion). "We may have to make a quick exit."

In my experience, though diner waitresses aren't likely to be asked out by royalty, they've not only pretty much seen it all and aren't easily thrown, they often have kind hearts as well.

"Sure, honey." She tore a sheet of paper from her pad. "Just leave it on the table."

"Now all we have to do is wait," I said to Ella. "When the movie guys go, we follow them out." What could be easier?

For once it really was as easy as I thought it would be – at least to start with.

We sipped our tea in companionable silence until Ella leaned across the table and said, "Lola! They're getting ready to go."

"Really? What are they doing?"

"They just gave the waitress their money,"

reported Ella. "Now they're standing up."

"Right." I took some money from my pocket and stuck it under our bill. "Be ready to move!"

"Here they come!" whispered Ella.

I watched the two men pass us. I watched them open the door of the diner. I watched them step outside.

I gave the command. "That's it! Let's go!"

We slipped from our booth and went after them.

Ella had her hand on the door, and I had my eyes on the backs of the two men as they crossed the street, when someone accustomed to screaming over the sound of drills and engines shouted my name so loudly that a hush fell over the Dellwood Diner and all eyes turned to us. Ella, who isn't as accustomed to thinking on her feet as I am, froze. Which meant I froze, too.

It was all I could do not to wail out loud, "Oh ye gods! Why does everything go wrong for me?"

"Lola!" Mr Creek shouted again. "Wait up!"

I looked over my shoulder, smiling with delighted surprise.

"Oh, Mr Creek! Hi!"

Mr Creek slid off his stool with the grace of a man whose tango is a New Jersey legend and moved towards me. "Lola, I was just talking about you."

"I'm really sorry, Mr Creek, but I'm kind of in a hurry." I gave Ella a shove.

Mr Creek gestured vaguely behind him. "But I wanted—"

118

"I'm really sorry, but I can't now." I edged myself through the door. "It's an emergency. Ella's mother just rang and a raccoon got into the house." This really did happen to someone in Dellwood, though not to Ella's mother of course. It's hard enough for micro-organisms to get into the Gerard house, never mind a largish mammal. I read about it in the local paper.

Mr Creek stopped. "But, Lola—"

"Next time!" I cried, waving wildly as I ran down the steps.

Ella was already on the pavement. "Well they didn't park on Main Street," said Ella. "There's no sign of them."

I started to run. "Quick! They must've parked behind the bank."

But there was no sign of them in the municipal parking lot behind the bank either.

"They must've been helicoptered out," I moaned as we started back down Main Street.

"Well, we tried," said Ella. "We came close."

Close, but no cigar. Not even the stub of a cigar.

Across the street, Mr Creek came out of the diner and climbed into his van. I pulled Ella into a doorway so he wouldn't see us loitering and wonder what the big rush had been for.

"It's all his fault," I muttered. "Why can't he eat breakfast at home like a normal person?"

The man Mr Creek was sitting next to at the counter came down the steps of the diner, gave him a wave, and got into the maroon people carrier in

119

the next space.

I've noticed that sometimes, when something really horrendous happens, to protect you from having a nervous breakdown your mind gets caught on some tiny, mundane detail. I got stuck on the fact that Mr Creek's breakfast companion had a really long nose. "Ella." I gave her a poke. "Ella, does that guy look familiar?"

"Only the back of his head looks familiar," said Ella.

We were too far away and the sun was in our eyes, but I felt like I'd seen him before… you know, like maybe he worked in the supermarket or something.

"No, really. Isn't he the manager of Food City?"

Mr Creek pulled out of his space and started up Main Street, and the maroon car followed.

"Like you care, right?" said Ella.

"It's just that I—"

The people carrier was right in front of us, and I could finally see the driver clearly.

A soul-ripping cry (not dissimilar to that of a mother gorilla watching her baby being carried off by poachers) shattered the dull quiet of the Dellwood morning.

Ella jumped. "For God's sake! Now what's wrong?"

"Oh, Ella!" I pointed after the vanishing New York number plate. "That was Charley Hottle!"

As If Enough Things Aren't Going Wrong, Sam Turns Against Me

As soon as I'd recovered sufficiently from my shock, horror, disappointment and frustration, I called Sam to see if he wanted to go to a movie that night.

He jumped at the chance.

"I thought you'd forgotten all about me," said Sam. "We're a little stretched right now, so I'll pick you up at seven-thirty."

Another thing experience has taught me is that nothing is ever as straightforward as it seems. Not even me. Although I'd been so busy that I hadn't even spoken to Sam since we went to Triolo's and was really looking forward to seeing him, missing Sam wasn't the main reason I asked him to go out. Just because I had actually been in the same room as Charley Hottle and had (stunningly) missed my opportunity to introduce myself didn't mean it was all bad news. Maybe when Mr Creek said he'd just been talking about me, he meant he'd been talking about me to Charley Hottle. Maybe as he'd passed the ketchup Mr Creek had said, *You know my boy's girlfriend is a terrific actor.* Maybe when Mr Creek said he wanted something what he'd wanted was to introduce me to a Hollywood icon. *Charley, old buddy, this is the girl I was telling you about.* At the very least I expected that, since Mr Creek and Charley Hottle were on a waving-goodbye basis, he might have some useful information to pass on to Sam.

"So," I said once I'd wedged myself into Sam's car, "did your dad tell you I saw him in the diner this morning?"

Sam said, "No."

Personally, I think it's totally astounding that it was men who invented telephones, televisions and computers, since on a day-to-day level they're so abysmally bad at communicating.

"No?" I laughed just in case he was actually joking. "He didn't mention me?"

Sam shook his head. "Nope."

"Just what do you and your father talk about all day?" I asked.

"What do you mean, 'what do we talk about'? We talk about cars."

[Cue: the hopeless, frustrated sigh of every woman who has ever tried to understand a man.] "You mean he didn't even say that he sat next to Charley Hottle at breakfast?"

"You don't mean Charley Hottle the director, do you?" Sam gave me a thoughtful look. "Is that why you asked me to go to the movies? To pump

122

me about *him*?"

I bristled with indignation. "Of course not. I missed you. I feel like I haven't talked to you in ages. We've got a lot to catch up on."

To get us off the obviously delicate subject of Charley Hottle, I told him what had been happening while we drove to town. I guess there must've been even more to tell than I thought because when Sam stopped in front of the cinema to let me out while he parked the car, he suddenly interrupted me right in the middle of a sentence and said, "Am I ever going to get a chance to say anything or is tonight going to be a one-woman show?"

I thought he was kidding. "You said all you talk about is cars."

Sam leaned his head against the window and gave me his who's-been-stripping-the-gears look. "With you I don't even get to talk about that. I just about get to say 'Hi' and then you're off on one of your monologues."

People always say that artists can be temperamental, but in my experience mechanics can be just as moody. "What are you so grouchy about? Bad day in the world of automotive repairs?"

"I don't have any trouble with engines," said Sam. "I understand them. You're what I don't understand. I haven't spoken to you for two days and you don't even ask me how I am. You don't even think I might have something interesting to say unless it's about some guy who sat with my old man in the diner. It's all blah, blah, blah, blah, blah, welcome to the Lola Cep Show."

I felt he was being crushingly unfair. "Oh excuse me if I've been boring you, Mr Creek. Maybe if we limited ourselves to carburetors—"

"You were boring me into a coma."

"In that case I'll shut up for the rest of the night, shall I?" I clamped my mouth closed and opened the passenger door.

"I don't want you to shut up completely. I just want you to shut up about this dumb movie." He gave me a poke. "Please."

A great actor has to be able to admit her faults or she never corrects them, she just keeps on repeating them, so I could accept that in my determination to be in the movie I may have been just a teeny bit self-obsessed. Besides, my rule is to never hold grudges because it makes your soul small and sour and interferes with fulfilling your true creative potential. (The only exception I make to this rule is Carla Santini.) On the other hand, I didn't want to give in too easily. I started to move, silent and chin held high.

Sam reached over and grabbed my shoulder, almost tenderly for someone used to gripping a wrench. "I'll pay for the popcorn."

Who could stay mad with an offer like that? "And the drinks," I said as I climbed out.

I stood in front of the cinema to wait for Sam. I'd more or less promised not to *talk* about the movie, but that didn't mean I couldn't think about it. I was actually wondering if maybe I should forget about it (not in a serious way of course – just in a *what if?* way, to see if that idea profoundly depressed me, which it did) when the door to the wine store across the street opened and a young man wearing dark glasses and a Panama hat stepped out. It was the hat that caught my attention; men from Dellwood do not wear Panama hats (unless maybe they're middle-aged and on vacation in Panama). And then he smiled to himself. It was a nuke-your-heart smile I'd seen dozens of times on the covers of magazines and on the big screen. *Good Lord!* I cried silently. *It's Bret Fork!*

He turned right and started walking to where he must've left his car.

In my experience, Fate's pretty stingy and doesn't hand out second chances very often. This time I didn't hesitate – not for the smallest fraction of a second. I went after him.

It was a balmy summer evening and the man the newspapers called Hollywood's strongest babe magnet wasn't in a hurry. He strolled along, whistling an old Beatles' song and swinging the Dellwood Wines bag he was carrying in a happy-go-lucky way, and I followed at a discreet distance – close enough to keep pace, but not close enough to make him feel that he was being followed. We didn't have far to go. His car – a black four-by-four to go with his rugged, masculine image (he does a lot of thrillers) – was parked in front of the gourmet deli. He unlocked it with an electronic beep, but instead of getting in he suddenly turned and went into the store.

In New York or Hollywood you wouldn't leave your car unlocked while you ran around to the back to get something out of the boot, but Dellwood is the kind of town that inspires an old-fashioned lack of caution. I figure it's the tree-lined streets and white clapboard churches – it makes you think you're in a really old Judy Garland movie. Whatever, Dellwood definitely inspired an old-fashioned lack of caution in me. Which is the only way I can explain what I did next.

One minute I was hovering at the edge of the deli's window, watching Bret Fork choose butter cookies from the bakery counter; and the next I was slipping into the back of his car and hunkering down on the floor.

Since I'd acted spontaneously (an ability that is as important in life as it is on the stage), this was one time when I didn't really have a plan. I just thought that if I could have a few minutes alone with him I'd be able to convince him to use his influence to get me a small part waving to my sisters on the school bus or something like that.

Bret Fork was still whistling when he got into the car. He started the engine, and pulled into the road as he punched a number into his cell phone.

"Hi," he said. "It's me... Of course I'm still coming. If I don't get out of that house I'll go nuts... I feel like I'm being haunted. There haven't been that many princesses under one roof since the last royal wedding. [Cue: sour laugh.] Yeah, right … anyway, I need the directions again… [Cue: grunting and sound of pen on paper.] What's it called? Bergstrom's…? OK… See you soon…"

Bergstrom's! Oh my God! Bergstrom's Travel Lodge! It was understandable that I'd forgotten all about it – most of the world had. Bergstrom's is zillions of miles out of town off the old highway. I'd only passed it a couple of times and it didn't even look open. That must be where the crew was staying. I was so excited I could feel my blood bubbling. This was it! Bret Fork was about to drive me right into the heart of the movie camp. At last my destiny was reaching out to me in a positive kind of way.

But not for long.

I guess I must've been even more excited than I thought – excited enough to make some sound that stood out against the steady rumbling of the engine – because as we stopped at a light Bret said, "What's that?"

Needless to say I didn't answer. But this precaution did me no good. I could hear him unsnap his seatbelt and heave himself up to peer over the back of his seat.

I looked up, my eyes round and innocent as Bambi's. It didn't work.

For a second or two he just stared back at me, and then he started yelling. "Effin' crazy fans! Who the hell are you? Have you been stalking me? Where did you come from?"

You have to be careful with people who are hysterical, especially if they're normally emotional and temperamental (which I figured movie actors are if Lucy Rio was anything to go by). I pulled myself up from the floor, reasonable and calm. "I'm not crazy," I quickly assured him. "And I'm not a fan. I mean I am a fan – I've seen tons of your movies. But I don't want an autograph or a lock of your hair or anything like that. And I definitely wasn't stalking you. I just happened to—"

"Then what is it you want?" he bellowed. "What the hell are you doing in my car?"

"Nothing." My voice was soothing and kind. "I just want to talk to you."

The light changed to green, but Bret Fork was still staring at me and didn't notice. (He didn't look nearly as handsome close up as he did in pictures – especially with his face that colour.) Horns started honking behind us.

"The light's changed," I informed him. "Maybe you should move."

He finally decided to pay some attention to what I was saying. He went as far as the kerb and then he stopped again. "Out!" he ordered. "Get out of my car."

"But Bret – Mr Fork – If you'd only listen for a minute—"

He leaned over his seat and opened the passenger door with much more force than you'd expect from a man who was twisted in such an awkward position – I was a little surprised that the

128

handle didn't come off in his hand. "Out!"

"But Mr Fork, you don't understand. It's my mother. She's ill. She's very ill. Terminally ill. I just thought if I could have the tiniest little part in your movie – in a crowd – even at the back of a crowd – at least I'd know that she'd gone to her death proud of me and knowing I was going to be all—"

"I'm telling you one more time." He'd taken out his cell phone again and was shaking it in my face. "If you don't get out of this car, I'm calling the cops."

I'm not really afraid of being arrested. I mean, many great people have done time. Ghandi was in jail. Martin Luther King was in jail. Nelson Mandela spent most of his life behind bars. And according to my history teacher, Eugene Victor Debs even ran for President of the United States from prison. So I'd be in good company. But I wasn't ready for the clanging shut of the cell door just yet. And I knew from my extensive experience of Karen Kapok that it's impossible to reason with someone in such a totally irrational and agitated state as the one Bret Fork was in. I got out of the car.

I was still standing there, watching the empty road (well, empty of Bret Fork and his four-by-four) when Sam screeched to a halt in front of me. He looked pretty agitated, too.

"Lola! What are you doing?" He opened the passenger door. "I've been going crazy. I thought something'd happened to you."

I squashed myself into the Karmann Ghia while

129

I started to explain what I was doing a mile from the movie.

"Hang on! Hang on! Back up the truck." I could see that the look of stricken concern with which Sam had been gazing at me had changed to something more like awe. "Are you saying that I finally get to see you and you leave me standing on the street like a jerk while you *followed* some dumb movie star, and then when he was in the deli you hid in his car? Is that what you're saying?"

Maybe the look on his face wasn't awe; maybe it was horror.

"You don't have to take it personally." I tried to explain. "It's not like I planned it. It just happened. You know, like spontaneous combustion. I was going to come back."

Sam shook his head in the way of a mechanic who has tried everything but who is going to have to scrap the car. "You just don't know when to stop, do you?" He started the engine. "You go though the give way signs. You go through the red lights. I bet you don't even see the yellow lights." He pulled into the road.

"Oh for God's sake. It's not like I was going to hurt him or anything. I just wanted to – hey!" I tapped Sam on the shoulder. "You're going the wrong way. The movie's back there."

"I don't feel like the movie now. I'm taking you home," said Sam. "You may not know when to stop, but I do."

I Go Through Another
Give Way Sign

I got Sam to drop me off at Ella's so I could discuss recent events in the privacy I never get at home but sorely deserve.

Ella was surprised to see me. "What are you doing here? I thought you were going to the movies with Sam."

I explained about Sam's irrational mood swings.

Ella said I never ceased to amaze her. "You have more balls than the Yankees and no conscience as far as I can see. If I'd treated someone like that I'd be racked with guilt, but you don't seem very upset."

I wasn't. I knew Sam would get over being mad at me pretty fast. He's a mechanic, after all. It's a very Zen profession. They don't get hung up on minuscule, transient things. Besides, deep down, Sam wouldn't really want me to change my nature – and my nature is spirited and unpredictable. That's what he loves about me. It'd be like getting a lion so you could keep it in a cage.

"Let me worry about Sam. Right now I have other, far more pressing things on my mind."

"Oh really? Like what?"

[Cue: dramatic pause of great detective about to name the killer.] "I found out where the film crew's staying."

Sometimes Ella blooms under my tutelage and sometimes she reverts to her more cautious and repressed self.

"But you can't be sure that they're staying at Bergstrom's," she said when I told her. "I mean, maybe it's just his girlfriend's staying there."

"And why would she do that? Why wouldn't she stay with him at the Santinis'?"

"OK, maybe not his girlfriend. Maybe just a pal."

"Oh, please. He's come here to work, not go fishing. And anyway, so what if I'm not sure? Nothing in this life is certain, is it? But there's a good chance that I'm right. I mean, they do have to be somewhere – and they aren't anywhere else that I could find."

Ella gave me the kind of look those with limited imaginations and the tendency to be easily discouraged often give those who are creative, bold and non-accepting of petty limits and defeats (you know, wary).

"So what are you planning to do now?"

"*We're* going to go over to Bergstrom's tomorrow evening and introduce ourselves to Charley Hottle, that's what I'm planning to do."

Ella was shaking her head like one of those dogs in the back window of a car. "Oh, I don't know, Lola. What if he recognizes us from when we were thrown off the set?"

You can understand why visionaries and revolutionaries get pretty frustrated. The number of times some people have to be told the same thing before they get it is no less than stupefying. "We've been through this. He isn't going to recognize us. We look totally different when we're clean and dry and intact."

[Cue: sour face and ten-ton sigh.] "So I take it you want me to drive us there," said Ella.

Mrs Magnolia was glad to see me the next morning, even though she hadn't exactly been rushed off her feet in my absence.

"It's this movie," judged Mrs Magnolia. "It's turned the whole town upside down. Do you know it took me forty-five minutes to get home last night because Lucy Rio was signing autographs in the shopping centre and it caused a traffic jam? Can you imagine? The only time we've ever had a traffic jam around here before was when the sewer backed up and flooded the main road."

I sympathized. "It's crazy, isn't it? So much ado about nothing."

"Even Mr Magnolia's getting carried away. If he polishes that car any more he's going to wear a hole right through it." She sighed. "I never thought I'd hear myself say this, but I think you and I may be just

133

about the only two level-headed people left in town."

Ella picked me up after work.

Bergstrom's Travel Lodge is a large, sprawling, two-storey brick building that looks vaguely colonial (there's a clock tower and a rooster weathervane on top of that), which was obviously constructed in more hopeful times. You know, when someone for some reason thought New Jersey was going to become the tourist hot spot of the eastern seaboard.

"Wow..." breathed Ella as we pulled off the highway. "I've never seen it so full before. It looks like a car auction."

"I don't see the equipment trucks, though. Maybe they're still on the set." I unfastened my seatbelt. "Come on, let's go and make sure that Charley Hottle's registered."

The lobby continued the colonial theme (rounded wooden chairs and tables, brass lamps, a fake fireplace complete with coalscuttle and upholstery featuring eagles and flags). At the very back was a high, polished, wooden counter with a sign on the front that said, "Bergstrom's – Where the Journey Is as Important as the Destination". There was a hallway on either side of the lobby, and the door to one of them was propped open with a cleaner's cart, but there was no sign of a maid and no one behind the reception desk.

"Hello?" I called. "Hello? Is anybody here?"

Ella surveyed the desk. "Isn't there usually a bell or something?" There was half a cup of coffee and a large, black book that was obviously the register next to the computer, a pink sweater over the back of the high, swivel chair behind it, and three phones on the counter, but no bell.

"It's sort of eerie, isn't it?" whispered Ella. "It's like they've been abducted by aliens or something."

"Except that I can hear footsteps above us." And the opening and closing of doors somewhere else in the building. I called again, "Hello? Hello?" When no one answered I leaned over the desk and turned the register around.

"Lola!" hissed Ella. "Lola, what are you doing?"

"What does it look like I'm doing? I want to see if Charley Hottle's checked in here."

"But you can't do that. It's private." Ella is not only my best friend, she likes to double as the conscience she says I don't have.

I flipped back a few pages and found one that had Plentitude Productions written at the top. I wanted to shout and sing and jump up and down. I wanted to run onto the roof and scream to the sky and the sun and the passing cars: *I was right! I was right! I knew I was right!* But all I said was, "If it's so private they shouldn't leave it lying around like that." My eyes ran down the page like a mouse down a wall.

I'd just spotted Charley Hottle's name (room 65) when a woman suddenly appeared down the hallway to our left and started banging on one of the doors. "Gracia!" she shouted. "Gracia! Hurry up! Aren't you done yet? Paloma needs some help upstairs."

135

"*Pero* Mrs Seiser," Gracia shouted back. "There is throw-up beneath the bed. I need more cloths."

"I suppose we should be grateful it isn't a body," snapped Mrs Seiser. "I'll get some rags."

Ella jumped at this intrusion, but I calmly shut the book and was leaning with my back to the counter by the time Mrs Seiser came marching towards us like an invasion.

I've lived long enough with Karen Kapok to know when someone is eyeing me suspiciously. "Who are you looking for?" she demanded.

"The manager. We—"

"That's me." I hid my surprise. Mrs Seiser's general demeanour seemed better suited to the job of prison guard than hotel manager. "I'll be with you in a second."

The phone started ringing as she strode past us to the opposite hallway. "Get that for me, will you? If it's someone wanting a room before August, tell them we're all booked up. If it's someone wanting to speak to one of the guests, they're all out so they'll have to call back later."

I picked up the phone. I'd seen enough movies with hotels in them to be able to do this cold. "Bergstrom's Travel Lodge, where the journey is as important as the destination," I said in my most businesslike voice. "May I help you? Just wait one minute please and I'll check... Oh, I'm so sorry, I'm afraid we're fully booked at the moment. Perhaps you'd care to make a reservation for later in the summer ... or even in the autumn? That's a spectacular time of year in New Jersey – when the entire countryside looks like it's dressed in a coat of many colours."

Ella poked me in the ribs. "Stop ad-libbing!" she hissed. "You don't work here, you're just answering the phone."

I turned my back on her. A great actor can't let the audience distract her. "Thank you so much for choosing Bergstrom's," I purred. "Please call again when your path next takes you past our door."

Ella groaned as I put down the receiver. I told her she sounded like the pipes in our house. She told me I sounded like some kind of New Age salesperson.

"I'm surprised you didn't ask their star sign," said Ella.

"And I'm surprised yours isn't the crab."

The phone had just started ringing again when Mrs Seiser rematerialized carrying a bucket and some rags.

"Don't worry, I'll get it," I called.

"Thanks." She held up her hand. "Just a few more seconds..." She charged past us and disappeared through the door where Gracia had found throw-up under the bed.

"She seems pretty busy," said Ella. "I guess they're not used to so much business."

I said, "Um..." I was watching the door in case Charley Hottle suddenly walked through it, but though my mind wasn't forming conscious thoughts, deep down below the surface, where creativity and instinct meet to become genius, it was engaged in serious thinking. It does that kind of thing all the time.

Mrs Seiser finally came back again.

"I'm sorry." She continued briskly past us. "But I'm having one of those summers. These people really think that they're the centre of the solar system. You've been very helpful, for which I am grateful, but if you're here because of the movie I—"

This is where the creativity and instinct meet to make genius bit comes in. Without any of the work or trouble of conscious thought I said, "Movie?" I gazed at the back of her head in innocent surprise. "I'm sorry..." My voice was hesitant and polite. I didn't want to be rude to an adult of course, but I was genuinely confused. "I'm afraid I don't know what you're talking about."

Mrs Seiser stopped as though there was a white rhino in her path. She turned to look at me. "You don't?" Her eyes moved from me to Ella and back to me. "Are you saying you two don't know they're making a Hollywood movie nearby and that the film crew's staying here? I thought everybody within a hundred mile radius knew that."

"Really? *Here?*" I fairly clapped my hands in girlish glee. I turned to Ella. "Wow, did you hear that? They're making a movie in Dellwood! And we didn't hear a word about it!" I turned back to Mrs Seiser. "How exciting for you to have the crew in your hotel!"

Mrs Seiser sighed a nothing-is-all-good kind of sigh. "I suppose so. But they've pretty much taken us over and it's – well, it's a little stressful." She stepped behind the reception desk. "But enough of that, since you aren't here because you want to talk to the producer or the director or ask the soundman about his equipment like everyone else in the county, what can I do for you?"

Ella looked at me – expectation mingled with fear of the unknown.

I smiled back at Mrs Seiser, knowing exactly what I was going to say. "My friend and I are looking for summer jobs."

I could tell from the way her eyes were practically popping out of her head that my friend had stopped breathing.

"Oh..." Mrs Seiser murmured. It was a weakly hopeful sound. "Well, I *could* use a couple of extra chambermaids – just while these movie people are here, you understand..." She looked us up and down. I prayed she couldn't tell that Ella lived in an exclusive community where everyone had servants. "I don't suppose you have any experience?"

It's important to be trusted by your employer of course, so I shook my head in an honest, forthright manner. "Not in this large an establishment," I admitted. "But my mother used to have a bed and breakfast when we lived in Connecticut, and naturally I helped her out."

Ella made a sound that was somewhere between choking and gurgling but Mrs Seiser was umming approvingly and didn't hear her. "You don't say... Well that counts as experience in my book." She

139

glanced over at Ella. "And what about you?"

Ella did her impersonation of a rabbit caught in headlights.

"Ella's mother has very exacting standards of neatness and cleanliness," I explained, "so though she has no professional experience as such you would have to consider her trained."

Desperation is a very powerful incentive, and if anyone was desperate it was Mrs Seiser. "Well," she said, "I don't suppose there's any harm in giving you a try." She laughed, a sound as close to happiness as hell is. "At least you speak English." She opened a drawer and took out two sheets of paper. "Why don't you take these application forms with you and fill them out tonight. If you come around eight tomorrow morning after the Hollywood mafia's left for the day, we'll get you started straight away."

"Thank you," I said. "You won't regret this."

Mrs Seiser gave another sad laugh. "Let's hope you don't."

It wasn't until we were back in the car that Ella finally spoke.

"Crazy," she said. "You are definitely, absolutely and without any qualifications, one hundred and fifty per cent certifiably insane."

And people think *I* exaggerate. I'm strictly an amateur next to Ella. "Well, I think I'm pretty brilliant."

"Oh, do you?" Ella jabbed the key into the ignition as if it was a knife. "And what do you think is so brilliant? Getting us jobs as maids without even consulting me? Is that your definition of brilliance?"

"Oh, come on, El. This is our golden opportunity. It's way better than just waltzing in and asking to see him. We'll be there every day. Which means we're bound to run into him in a casual, non-threatening way. It'll be like taking candy from a sleeping baby. We'll say 'hi', and he'll say 'hi'. We'll exchange pleasantries about the weather. He'll ask us for extra towels, and we'll ask him if we can be extras. If you ask me, it's like a present from the gods."

One Gerard eyebrow rose in disdain. "Oh, really? You don't think that maybe you're overlooking one or two things? Like my mother? What's my mother going to say when I tell her what we're doing? Do you think she's going to race to the phone to tell all her friends? 'Oh! Guess what! My daughter's got a job as a maid!'?"

"They wouldn't believe her. Your mom's friends think all maids are Hispanic."

"Hahaha. Answer my question."

"Oh for Pete's sake." It never ceases to amaze me how people like Ella always have to create problems where none exist. "So don't tell her."

"What do you mean, 'don't tell her'? You don't think she might notice that I'm out of the house before she gets up and don't come home all day?"

Even I could see that this was ridiculous. Unlike Karen Kapok, Mrs Gerard has a very hands-on attitude to motherhood. But once you're firmly set on the path of brilliance you just keep going, don't you? "OK." I nodded towards the building next to

141

Bergstrom's. "Tell her we're working in the diner. It's so close it's not really a lie." Mrs Gerard is a woman who makes her own pasta. She was more likely to become a chambermaid herself than drop by the diner to check.

Ella groaned. I had her cornered. "All right. Let's say she buys that, what about the other little things you've so conveniently forgotten? Like the fact that you already have a job? And the fact that we don't know what our hours or responsibilities are or even what they're paying us?"

I considered these to be tediously trivial details. "Who cares what they're paying us or anything like that? We're not in it for the money, El. And as far as my other job goes, it's not a big deal. I'll just tell Mrs Magnolia that Karen's having cash-flow problems and I need to get something that pays more. I'll tell Karen that Mrs Magnolia had to lay me off because business is so bad." I could work on an assembly line for all my mother cared, as long as I got paid.

I've heard Ella's mother sigh in exactly the same way when the cream sauce curdled.

"You can't actually be a pathological liar," said Ella, "because I don't think a pathological liar knows that she's lying."

"And as for the other stuff," I went on, "what does it matter?"

"What does it matter?" parroted Ella. "I'll tell you what it matters. For one thing, I'm not sure I'm up to hard manual labour. I read this book about low-wage workers and—"

"Ella, we're not building the pyramids here." I laughed. "We're just making a few beds and putting fresh towels and soap in the bathrooms. What could be easier than that? And anyway, it's not like it's a career move. It's a temporary measure. As soon as we get our parts, we quit. And there's no way we won't get parts now. We're practically living with the crew."

"So is Carla," said Ella, "but she doesn't have to clean their toilets."

Somehow, I hadn't thought about cleaning toilets being involved. I shoved the thought aside.

"You're being negative. It's not like you'll have to even look. They'll have the latest toxic chemical to do the work for you. And besides, you have to view this from the right perspective. This is an important rite of passage for us."

Ella looked over as she put the car in reverse. "Being maids?"

"Only in a general sense. I mean joining the real workforce. Let's face it, you and I have led sheltered lives, Ella. You especially. But now we're officially no longer children – and, as the poet said, it's time to put away childish things. If you think about it, this is a much bigger step than just going to college. School is not reality, Ella. This is our chance to see what adult life is really like."

"You're already part of the workforce," Ella reminded me.

"But not one where the rest of the staff speaks Spanish."

As Rites Of Passage Go,
This One Isn't As Good
As A Wedding

My confidence in dealing with the first group of minor details wasn't misplaced.

When I told Mrs Magnolia that there were hard times in the world of handmade dinnerware that made it imperative for me to make more money than she was giving me, she was as philosophical as you might expect of someone who is plagued by migraines and who works in used clothes.

"The small business is an endangered species in this country," she said. "Tell your mother she has my sympathy."

I said I knew my mother would appreciate that.

When I told Karen I had a job as a chambermaid she said, "You? The girl who thinks the floor is an extension of her closet?"

I told her I'd heard of many professional gourmet chefs who eat baked beans and frozen dinners at home. "A job is different to life," I said.

"That's what you think," said my mother.

Ella picked me up at seven-thirty the next morning. We were silent all the way to the travel lodge because Ella wasn't capable of speech yet and wasn't willing to listen to mine.

A maroon people carrier was pulling out of the parking lot as we pulled in.

"Look!" I cried. "It's Charley Hottle! We just missed him!"

"Don't scream like that," Ella ordered. "I nearly went into shock."

At last, the wall of hostility that Fate had constructed around me was starting to crumble. "Oh, this is so definitely the break we needed. I wonder how long our shift is? Maybe we'll still be here when he gets back."

Ella pulled into a space that said Employee Parking. "If we are I hope we're getting overtime," she grumbled.

It was barely eight o'clock and already Mrs Seiser looked like she'd had a long, hard day. She sounded like it too.

"It's one thing after another with these movie people," she informed us as soon as we stepped into the lobby. "They never stop. Where's this? Where's that? Why can't you? Why didn't you? What happened to? Yadayadayada morning, noon and night. They must all have servants." Mrs Seiser sniffed. "Servants or slaves. And of course Gracia's cousin Paloma's supposed to be helping us out, but she didn't turn up at all today." She lowered her voice to a confidential level. "Those people are so unreliable. They have no sense of loyalty and commitment." She gave another disapproving sniff. "And of course they don't really like to work. You have to keep on them every minute."

I wasn't sure which people she was talking about – maids? People who are helping you out? Women named Paloma? – but I stood up tall and smiled confidently so that she'd know I wasn't to be counted among their number. "We can't wait to get started," I assured her. "We're both imbued with a very strong work ethic."

"It's nice to know someone is," said Mrs Seiser. "And thank God you've got some experience, I don't have even a few seconds this morning for a heavy training session. I've got to go and see what happened to the laundry. Come on, I'll go through the formalities and then Gracia will show you where everything is. If you have any questions, ask her."

The formalities included giving us algae-green housecoats, plastic nametags, yellow rubber gloves, and ticking off our duties on her fingers – twice.

Up until the moment Mrs Seiser handed me my nametag it had never occurred to me that it was possible to misspell "Lola".

"It doesn't matter," said Mrs Seiser. "We know who we mean."

Then she gave us each a photocopy of her own original composition: RULES FOR CLEANERS.

146

Mrs Seiser has more rules than the Old Testament. Don't do this ... don't do that ... don't even think about doing *that*... Just about the only thing a cleaner was allowed to do besides work was breathe.

"Any questions?" asked Mrs Seiser when she was done.

I cleared my throat. "I was just wondering... What about our breaks?"

Mrs Seiser's employees' smile wasn't as welcoming as her possible-guest smile. "Excuse me?"

I repeated my statement. "Isn't it a law that we get at least two breaks a shift?"

"Oh, of course." Mrs Seiser looked down at the sheet of paper in her hand. "Isn't it there?"

I shook my head. "I don't see it."

"Well it should be there." She made it sound like it was my fault that it wasn't. "Two fifteen-minute breaks and a half hour for lunch."

"We got an hour for lunch at school."

Mrs Seiser allowed her lips to part very slightly so I'd think she was smiling. "This isn't school."

"Well, that should make you happy," muttered Ella.

Mrs Seiser got up from her desk. "If there aren't any more questions, it's time you two— Lola? You've got *another* question?"

"Where's the staff room?"

"Excuse me?" I'd never really realized before how threatening politeness can be.

"The staff room." I smiled an eager, good-employee kind of smile. "You know … where we take our breaks? Rule 12 says we're not allowed to loiter on the premises. And Rule 11 says we're not allowed to eat, drink or smoke on the premises either."

"You can go to the diner next door."

I opened my mouth. "But—"

Mrs Seiser gave me a stern look. "I hope you're not going to be a trouble-maker, Lola. I gave you this job out of the goodness of my heart. Gracia does have other relatives, you know."

I think I may have seen too many movies featuring señoritas with dark, flashing eyes, long black hair, rustling skirts and shawls because Gracia didn't look anything like I expected. She was in her forties, her hair was short and blonde, her eyes were blue, her glasses were thick, and she wore jeans, a faded Lakers sweatshirt and trainers from somewhere like Shoe City.

"Not Mexico," she corrected me. "From Colombia."

Gracia's husband had been killed by para-militaries.

"What was he, some kind of guerrilla?" asked Ella.

Gracia said no, he worked for Coca-Cola and was active in the union. After he was murdered she took the children and fled.

Gracia showed us where the supplies were kept

and instructed us on the most efficient way to do our tasks (bathroom, bedroom, vacuum the hall when you've done all the rooms).

"Don't you worry," said Gracia. "Once you get accustomed to the things, you'll be swimming like ducks."

"Do you really take your break in the diner?" I asked her.

"If you break it, you buy it," said Gracia.

"No, no, I didn't mean that." That was rule 17. "I meant a break from work. You know, a rest."

"No rests," Gracia informed me. "There is no time."

Although, technically, we were paid by the hour, you didn't leave until your allotted tasks were done.

"But then you get overtime," said Ella.

"Exacto," said Gracia. "That's when your time is over."

Because we were new, Gracia suggested that Ella and I do the rooms together until we'd had some practice.

"You do the ground and I'll do arriba," she said, and disappeared up the stairs.

It took me three attempts to open the first room with my electronic key, and when I did it wasn't worth all the trouble.

"Good God!" gasped Ella as we stepped inside. "Look at this place! It looks like a pigsty!"

My eyes went slowly around the room. It wasn't a big room, but it was full. The token chair was

149

piled with clothes, most of the bedding was on the floor, and there were dirty glasses, food containers and empty beer bottles on every available surface, including the floor.

"I think you're doing a grave injustice to the pigs of this world. They don't usually leave their condom wrappers lying around." I picked up the wrapper with my gloved hand. God knew where the contents of the wrapper was, but I for one was not going to look under the bed.

"It's unbelievable." Ella seemed to be frozen by the door with horror. "I mean, these are intelligent, professional people – not a bunch of kids who were raised by wolves. It's a good thing my mother never had to do this job. It would've killed her."

There was something disgusting floating in half a glass of beer.

"This job may not kill me," I said, "but I think it's definitely going to make me sick."

Ella's eyes turned to the bathroom door. "I'm afraid to look in there."

I didn't see how it could be worse than the bedroom.

"I'll toss you." I took a coin from my pocket. "Heads I do in here, tails you do it."

Armed with brushes, cloths and disinfectant, Ella went into the bathroom looking like Indiana Jones being lowered into a pit of snakes.

She was out again in under five seconds.

"I can't," she said, her face contorted with

disgust. "There are *hairs* in the shower and the toilet's filthy."

"Hairs?"

Ella nodded. "You know…" She looked like there was a skunk loose in the room.

"Oh," I sighed. "You mean *hairs*." This job was like being a housewife, only you didn't even get a card and a bunch of flowers for Mother's Day. "I don't suppose there's a hose in the cart."

"You and your rites of passage," muttered Ella. "Next time, let's try one of the other ones. Like getting married. At least people give you presents."

I took a deep breath to prepare myself for tackling the bathroom. "You'd still end up having to clean the toilet," I said.

The Longest Day

The thought that while I was scrubbing toilet bowls and emptying ashtrays, Carla Santini was swanning around the movie set, batting her eyelashes and simpering inanely at Bret Fork, would have been a galling one if I'd had any time for thought. But I didn't. Drudgery doesn't really lend itself to thinking. Do this ... then do this ... then do that ... over and over until if it weren't for the exhaustion and pain you'd think you were a robot.

By the time the last hygienically sealed glass was put in place, the last spread smoothed down and the hall vacuumed, our shift had been officially over for more than two hours.

"Can you believe that people used to work at least fourteen hours a day, six days a week?" asked Ella as we limped into the supply closet to put our cart away.

I shut the door behind us. "No." There wasn't

a single part of my body that didn't hurt. "Even my nails and hair are aching in sympathy."

Ella sighed as many a sweatshop worker must have sighed before her. "I can't decide what I hate most about this job. It could be cleaning the bathrooms." Ella wrinkled her nose. "Or it could be how disgusting some of the sheets are."

It was true that there was a lot to choose from, but as far as I was concerned there was no contest. "I know exactly what I hate most. Mrs Seiser."

Mrs Seiser was a combination of the Gestapo and the speaking clock. Every time you turned around there she was watching you with her beady eyes, pointing out everything you hadn't done, everything you'd done wrong and how much time it'd taken you to do it in. If you so much as leaned against a wall for a few seconds to catch your breath she acted like she'd found you asleep in one of the beds. If she gave me a nickel every time she told me that she was running a hotel not a summer camp, I'd have more money than I was likely to make in a week.

"I don't even have the strength to take off this stupid housecoat." Ella removed her bag from the shelf where she'd left it and hung it over her shoulder. "All I want to do is get home before I collapse."

"Me too." All I could think of was the bath I was going to have the minute I got in. I didn't care if both the twins had the worst case of diarrhoea in the history of Dellwood, New Jersey, I was barricading myself in and soaking till I looked like a raisin.

Ella locked the door after us and we started down the hall. "I'll go and get the getaway car while you put this back in the office." She handed me the key. "I'll meet you out front."

Ella strode into the lobby. She was obviously in a semi-catatonic state and oblivious to the world around her because she didn't look twice at the man coming into Bergstrom's as she was going out. I, however, being an actor, always have a part of me alert no matter how many toilet bowls I've cleaned. I recognized Charley Hottle instantly, and no sooner did I recognize him than I turned around and went back the way I'd just come. I was suddenly wide awake again of course. Adrenaline coursed through my veins; my cells tingled. Ella disappeared, but I stayed at the entrance to the hallway, my eyes on Charley Hottle as he spoke to Mrs Seiser and waited for his messages. I had his room number imprinted on my brain (65), so as soon as he turned from the counter I raced up the stairs to the second floor. I had to hope that he really didn't recognize me from the other day, but if he did I'd just have to talk fast.

Maybe I should have gone after Ella and not approached Charley Hottle at the end of a long, hard day. I was tired and I knew I didn't look my best. But a great actor has to be able to overcome such minor negativities. A great actor has to be ready to go on even if her hair is limp and she

154

smells like disinfectant.

I was strolling casually down the corridor as Charley Hottle appeared at the top of the stairs.

I gave him a smile.

He didn't give me one back, probably because he didn't actually look at me.

"Hi," I said.

He nodded as he marched past me.

Now I understood why private eyes and spies always disguise themselves as maids and waiters and things like that in movies. Because no one sees them unless they want something or have a complaint.

"Mr Hottle!" I turned and went after him. "Mr Hottle, if I could just have—"

He didn't look back as he got to his room. "If it's about that lamp, it was like that when I moved in."

"It's not about the lamp. It's—"

"I'm busy," he snapped. The door shut in my face.

I knocked politely but firmly. "Mr Hottle, if you'd only just listen—"

The door opened so suddenly that I nearly knocked on his nose. "No, you listen," his eyes moved to my nametag, "Lolla. If you don't leave me alone I'm going to file a formal complaint with the manager."

"But Mr Hottle, you don't understand."

Charley Hottle couldn't possibly have had a worse day than I had, but he wasn't in any mood

155

for negotiation.

"No, you don't understand. I'm trying to make a movie here, and all you're supposed to be doing is making the bed. You and I have nothing to discuss unless I need an extra towel or you forgot to empty the rubbish bin. *Comprende?*"

Comprende? Was I a less important person because I made beds instead of Hollywood movies? Didn't I breathe just like he did? Didn't I bleed? Wasn't I human?

Apparently not. He was about to slam the door in my face again when Mrs Seiser suddenly entered the scene, stage right.

"Lola!" She had a small parcel in her hand and was steaming down the corridor like a runaway train. She was in full Gestapo mode. "Lola, what are you doing here?"

Even though Mrs Seiser had probably made a few beds in her time, Charley Hottle was overjoyed to see her. "Mrs Seiser! What did I tell you about keeping your staff out of my hair?"

Mrs Seiser disarmed when she spoke to Charley Hottle. "Thank heaven I forgot to give you this downstairs," she purred. "I had no idea she was up here bothering you." She picked up her submachine gun and turned back to me. "Go and wait for me in the office, Lola. You and I have a few things to discuss."

Everybody always says that there are two sides to every story, but in my experience most people only listen to one.

156

"But Mrs Seiser – I—"

"You heard me. Now!" She put away the submachine-gun and spoke to Charley Hottle again. "Mr Hottle, I am so sorry. The only excuse I can make for her is that she's new. I'm sure you know how hard it is to get good staff nowadays."

I slunk downstairs. I could see Ella waiting in the car outside Bergstrom's as I walked to the office. She was sound asleep.

I was meek and apologetic when Mrs Seiser came back to the office of course.

"It wasn't what you think," I said. "I saw Mr – what did you say his name is? Hottle? I saw Mr Hottle drop a dollar and I just wanted to return it, that's all."

Mrs Seiser didn't believe me. She said she was very disappointed in me. She had higher hopes. I've learned in life that you're always disappointing someone, so that part didn't really bother me. The part that bothered me was when she docked me half a day's salary for breaking one of her rules.

"I hope that will teach you a lesson," said Mrs Seiser.

"It has," I said.

Next time I'd make sure I didn't get caught.

My Life Is A
Bruce Springsteen Song

Because my mother has no qualms about inflicting her lack of musical taste on her innocent children, I know every song Bruce Springsteen ever wrote by heart. And since working at Bergstrom's, I knew I was definitely living one. Only it wasn't "Born to Run" or anything like that – something fast and upbeat and full of hope. It was the one about working in a factory and having your life destroyed by the tedium and mindless subservience of your job.

I sat at the dinner table like a ghost (only forcing my hands to lift my fork from my plate to my mouth because I knew I needed whatever crumbs of nourishment I could get). Around me, the mindless chatter and laughter of the living, sheltered from the harsher truths of the universe, surrounded me like fog.

"Mary! Mary! Mary!"

The way Paula was shrieking suggested that

she'd been trying to get my attention for several minutes. I turned my head slowly towards her. Every movement of any muscle in my body was a painful effort.

"Guess what we did today?" asked Pam.

Not only does manual labour fatigue your body, it also fatigues your mind. I now understood why most of the great ideas and discoveries of mankind were made by middle and upper class men. Who else would have the time and energy required to think? Not some guy picking cotton or chipping away at the bowels of the earth from dawn to dusk. Not some woman scrubbing floors and clothes until her hands bled. After two days slaving away at the plantation known as Bergstrom's Travel Lodge, I was pretty much beyond caring about anything. Demoralization (as well as aches, pains and calluses) came with the job. If I'd had any time to think, I was too tired and dispirited to bother. I asked Gracia what made her get up every morning and go to work – day after day and year after year – and she said it was all the bills she had to pay.

But despite this, I made an effort to rally for the sake of my sisters. I felt that their innocence should be protected for as long as possible. They'd learn the truth about the world soon enough.

"You discovered life on Mars?"

There was a stereophonic sigh from the other side of the salad bowl.

"We went to see the movie," said Paula. "Oona

May took everybody in day camp."

"We met Lucy Rio and Bret Fork, too," chipped in Pam.

"We even met the director," added Paula.

Of course they did. Somebody had to – and it was definitely starting to look like it was never going to be me. The life of a chambermaid was so hard and unpleasant and so soul-destroying that I couldn't even muster the reserve of energy I'd need to pursue Charley Hottle. Not that I'd had any chance to. Even though Ella and I never left at four (like we were supposed to), since the time he slammed the door in my face the closest I'd come to Charley Hottle was seeing his name in the register. And since the time Charley Hottle slammed the door in my face, Mrs Seiser watched me like a hawk with its eyes on a baby rabbit. Any time someone from the movie company was around, she appeared behind them like a spectre – or maybe a witch – and made sure I didn't get near them.

But a good actor can, of course, feign an enthusiasm she doesn't actually feel. "Wow... That must've been exciting."

"It was," chimed in Pam. "It was really cool."

"And guess who else was there?" crowed Pam. "Carla Santini and a bunch of her friends."

[Cue: thud as heart drops to feet.] "Carla Santini?" Why was she always on the set? Didn't she have anything else to do?

Karen Kapok groaned in a way that I'm pretty

sure I'll always associate with motherhood. "Oh, God, just when you think it's safe to have a conversation…"

"Yeah," said Paula. "She's in the movie, too. She said to say hi."

I could see Carla smiling graciously at my sisters, the coven all tittering inanely behind her.

"What a lovely person she is," I murmured. "Mother Teresa is an Inquisition torturer by comparison."

Pam bit a carrot stick in half. "She said she'll see you at the party."

"What party?"

"How should we know?" demanded Paula. "She said you got an invitation."

"Well, I didn't."

My mother gave me a scornful look over a forkful of salad. "I told you you had mail. I can't open it for you, you know. It's against the law."

The only things that should be against the law are Carla Santini and her parties (not so much social occasions as publicity stunts).

"You'll have to excuse me," I sweetly replied. "I'm afraid the drudgery of my servitude make things like mail irrelevant – since I barely have the strength to read it."

"Do you want Pam to go all the way over to the phone table to get it?" asked my mother. "Since you probably don't have the strength to make it across the kitchen either."

*　　*　　*

161

I waited till after the dishes were done before I casually picked the ivory-coloured, linen envelope embossed with silver stars from the phone table and took it to my room. Then I lit some candles to scare off the evil spirits that would be released when I broke the seal on the envelope and sat on my bed. I opened the invitation slowly, as though it might explode (though a slow poison would be more Carla Santini's style). The invitation was also embossed with silver stars – they probably cost more than a maid at Bergstrom's makes in a week.

You almost have to feel sorry for Carla. It's like she was born in totally the wrong time. This is a girl who should've been hatching plots in seventeenth-century European courts or in ancient Rome or Egypt. There isn't a power-hungry monarch who ever lived who wouldn't have given her a job. *Carla, I need to start a war between King Mubble and King Hopstadter. Do you think you can do something? Of course [coos Carla] I have twenty minutes before lunch.* And think of all the fun she would've had ruining lives and cutting off heads – all the while acting like she had nothing on her mind but what pearls to wear to dinner. I'm serious about this. Expensive clothes and cars and having every tiny little thing you want for even half a second are nothing next to real power. I mean, anybody can *buy* things, all you need is the money. What does Carla Santini care if she gets another eight-hundred-dollar pair of shoes, when deep in her heart she must know that she was born to

162

manipulate and control people and events? Imagine how deliriously happy she'd be if, when she got into bed at night, she could say to herself: *I brought down two governments and threw five hundred peasants off their land – now that was a good day!* instead of: *Bought another dozen dresses and a gold bracelet today – what a bore.*

It was obvious to me that (once again) she'd engineered this party so she could pour buckets of salt into my wounds in front of an audience. It wasn't enough to send me the invitation she'd sent everyone else – announcing that the party was to send Carla off on her college career and to celebrate the completion of Dellwood's first movie. At the bottom she'd written with her own fair hand, *Can't wait to compare notes on the movie. You have to come! Everybody's going to be there. They're all looking forward to seeing you again!*

As soon as I read Carla's invitation, I called Ella.

"I wasn't going to mention it," said Ella. "When you didn't say anything I thought you weren't invited."

"I wish I wasn't." If only I had some previous, unbreakable engagement (speaking at the UN or dinner with Sofia Coppola for instance).

"Well, you don't have to go," said Ella.

"Oh, yes I do." This wasn't an invitation, it was a challenge. "Lola Cep never backs away from a challenge."

"I wouldn't worry about it," said Ella. "The

163

way Gruppenführer Seiser works us we'll be dead before the end of August anyway."

I hadn't had a single dream since I'd started at Bergstrom's. Even my subconscious was wiped out. But that night I dreamt I was in one of the rooms, trying to scrub bloodstains out of the carpet. (This had happened to Gracia.) It wouldn't come out (which was the only connection between Bergstrom's and Shakespeare that I could see). I scrubbed and scrubbed but it didn't even fade. And then Mrs Seiser started shouting for me. "Lola! Lola! What's taking you so long? You better be doing a good job. I've had complaints!" (This had happened to me.) I shouted back that I was almost done. I started rubbing so furiously at the stain that my own hands started bleeding. And then I heard footsteps marching purposefully down the beige carpet. "Lola!" barked Mrs Seiser. "Lola! Do you want me to fire you? Do you want the whole world to know that you don't even have what it takes to be a maid?" And then Mrs Seiser started to laugh. Only it wasn't Mrs Seiser's laugh, which was like somebody grating an iceberg. It was the clear, pure sound of hundreds of tiny glass bells tinkling in a mountain breeze. Mrs Seiser had turned into Carla Santini, the way people do in my dreams. Even though in the real world I absolutely refused to even look under a Bergstrom's bed, in the world of dreams I dove under it like a prairie dog scurrying into its hole. "Lola, where are you? You have to

164

come to my party. You're the guest of honour." I could just see Carla's Jimmy Choo shoes in the doorway. "You know, Lola, you can run, but you can never hide," she purred.

Oh yes I can... I whispered in my heart. *Oh yes I can...*

Those words: *Oh yes I can...* were still running through my head when the alarm went off and I opened my eyes. Since I joined the real workforce I hit the snooze button at least six times before I finally dragged myself out of bed, but this morning I leapt to the floor with a cry of unfettered joy! That was it! That was all I had to do!

I was going to have to drop Bruce Springsteen a note and point out a song he'd forgotten to write: "Born to Hide".

You Can Only Wonder Why Nothing Ever Goes The Way It Should

"I don't like it," said Ella. "This has got to be one of your craziest ideas yet."

I pulled a mop handle out of my back. We were in the first-floor supply closet at the time, which was the only place where a working girl could get five seconds of privacy or peace at Bergstrom's.

"I knew I shouldn't tell you. You never like anything."

Ella put on the Marilyn Gerard stern, is-that-a-smudge expression I'd seen so many trillions of times before. "What if you get caught?"

[Cue: the weary kind of sigh Jesus often used when the disciples were being really dense.] "But I'm not going to get caught. When Charley Hottle comes back I'll just be stepping out of the bathroom. I'll explain that we were understaffed today so I'm late finishing up."

"And then?"

"And then we'll chat for a few minutes. You

know, about how much I admire his work and his dedication to family values in this crass age of sex, exploitation and violence. And then I'll work my charm on him."

And if that didn't do the trick, I'd tell him about my mother's operation and how the doctors said she'd lost the will to live and how if she knew that I was going to be in a movie (the dream she had for herself in her lost youth before everything started to go so horribly wrong for her) I was sure that she'd try to survive at least long enough to see it.

"But what if Gruppenführer Seiser finds out? What about Gracia?"

"Gracia? How did Gracia get into this?"

"His room's on her floor, isn't it? She'll get into trouble."

Maybe the cleaning chemicals we used were affecting Ella's mind. "How can Gracia get into trouble when she doesn't know anything about it?"

"Mrs Seiser will blame her, that's how," snapped Ella. "She blames her for everything."

"That was before I started working here. Now she blames me." I shifted my weight to the foot that wasn't going numb. "And besides, by the time the worst happens – which it won't – the Gruppenführer will be gone and the night manager will be on duty. Charley Hottle doesn't usually get back before six or seven." Mr Wolsky, the night manager, was a boy scout compared to Mrs Seiser's Nazi general.

"And I have to do what?"

"Practically nothing. You just have to distract

167

her while I borrow back my pass key."

"Oh, Lola..."

"You don't even have to do it in person. Just call her on your cell phone. Say you think you left your watch in the employee's bathroom. Ask her to check if it's there, and if it is to lock it in the safe."

"All right." Ella said this grudgingly.

"And be waiting for me at seven. Park in front of the diner. If I get out sooner, I'll call you."

Ella sighed. "Sometimes I think it was a really great loss to the criminal world when you decided to go on the stage," she said.

The first part of my plan went exactly as it was supposed to – which I guess I should've taken as a warning. But I didn't. I watched Mrs Seiser answer the telephone. I watched her frown and heave her bosom and march off to the employees' bathroom. I was through the front door quick as a missile and into the office; and up the stairs before she returned, empty-handed.

Once inside Charley Hottle's room I just stood there for a few minutes, looking around. Like the rest of his crew, Charley Hottle was obviously used to having servants. Although the bed was perfectly made and the bathroom sparkled (Gracia is very good at her job), aside from that it looked like the coast of Florida after a hurricane. He must've left in a hurry that morning because there was stuff thrown everywhere and there was a notebook and a gold Rolex on the bedside table in a puddle of change.

I sat on the closed toilet seat, cleaner carrier at my feet, and took out the book I'd brought with me. I figured I was going to have a long wait.

But I didn't. I'd hardly opened my book when I heard someone fumbling at the door. Although a person less accustomed to the jolts and surprises of the gods might have panicked, I silently praised the person who installed the temperamental electronic lock system in Bergstroms, because if they'd used the old-fashioned kind with manual keys whoever it was would've been inside before I could think, let alone move. In the minute or so I did have to think while he or she tried to open the door, what I thought wasn't *Charley Hottle's back early*, but *It must be Mrs Seiser!* I blame Ella for this. Ella's the Johnny Appleseed of Doubt, sprinkling its seeds around with gay abandon and the worrier's chant of *What if? What if?* Despite my strong character, Ella's pessimism had had its effect. So because I knew for sure that the film crew never knocked off this early; and because I wouldn't put it past the Gruppenführer to have noticed a passkey was gone and be conducting a room-by-room search for the culprit; and because I could hear Ella saying, "Didn't I tell you this wouldn't work?" by the time the lock finally released I was in the closet.

I kept the door open a crack so I could see a figure walk past. It wasn't Mrs Seiser. It was a youngish man wearing a black T-shirt that said Plentitude Productions on the back in white. He went over to the bedside table, picked up the notebook and stuck the watch in his pocket. I was congratulating myself on having made the right decision because he'd obviously been sent to get things Charley Hottle had forgotten, when instead of leaving he sat down on the bed and picked up the phone. He called somebody called "Honey" – as in "Honey, I can explain." I could tell this was going to take some time, so I sat down.

Except for my two seconds on the toilet, it was the first time I'd been off my feet all day and my work-wracked body, grateful for the rest, must've passed out. I didn't remember falling asleep, but I remember waking up. It was the sound of heavy breathing that woke me. The closet door was shut so I was in total darkness, and at first I didn't know where I was or what the grunts and sighs were. There might've been a gorilla on the other side of the door for all I knew. And then I remembered I was in a closet at Bergstrom's, so that pretty much ruled out gorillas. The only animals allowed in were guide dogs.

It took me a few more seconds to realize I was in the middle of a Passionate Love Scene. My first thought was that I was in the wrong room. That kind of thing happens all the time (it definitely happens to *me* all the time). Had I misremembered the room number? Had I been so afraid that Mrs Seiser was suddenly going to materialize in the hall that I went through the wrong door? I mean, it couldn't be Charley Hottle I was listening to. I knew from a piece in the local paper that Mrs Hottle was back on their ranch in Colorado with the seven kids.

And a man who was always going on about family values and stuff like that wasn't going to be panting and grunting over some other woman, was he?

They moved away from the closet, and I moved on to Plan B. Plan B was getting out of there as soon as possible. Even if I had to simply stroll out of my hiding place in a cool and nonchalant manner, give them a pleasant smile and calmly sashay out the door. I figured they'd be too surprised to say or do anything, and by the time they did I'd have vanished from the hallway as if I'd been beamed up by Scotty.

They got pretty involved in kissing and murmuring on the other side of the room. I started to count down from twenty. When I hit zero I'd make my exit. Nineteen ... seventeen ... fifteen ... thirteen ... eleven ... nine...

I took a deep breath and reached for the doorknob.

Five ... three...

And then he said, "How about a drink, Lil? I've got a bottle of wine I was saving for just this occasion."

I wasn't in the wrong room. I recognized Charley Hottle's voice. Horror and surprise brought me back to the floor so fast I banged my head against the wall. Another thing I knew from the local paper was that Mrs Hottle's name is Tamara.

Once I recovered from my shock that Mr Family Values was messing around with a woman who wasn't his wife (so much for believing what you read in glossy magazines), I realized that although this

171

was obviously bad news for Mrs Hottle – and I did sympathize with her – it was even worse news for me. I couldn't very well just stroll out of the closet as if I'd wandered in there by mistake now. A man who's cheating on his wife isn't going to be happy to see a witness – especially someone as famous as Charley Hottle. He'd think I was going to run straight from his room to *The Enquirer* to sell my story.

Lil demurred. She'd had nothing but a bagel all day and was worried that the wine would go straight to her head.

"No room service in this dump of course, but maybe we can get a pizza delivered," suggested Charley Hottle.

Lil didn't feel like pizza. She was all pizzaed-out.

The next suggestion was Chinese food.

Lil worried that they hadn't heard how bad monosodium glutamate is for you in the New Jersey outback.

Good God, I thought. *I'm going to be here all night.* My stomach growled. Lil wasn't the only one who was running on empty.

Charley Hottle figured they could get the diner to send something over, but Lil wasn't too keen on the diner either.

"Well there is nowhere else." He wasn't murmuring any more. "I haven't got the car, remember?"

She finally gave in.

I rubbed the foot that had fallen asleep. What was I going to do? Aside from the fact that I was either going to starve to death or go into paralysis if I had to spend the night in the closet, what if he wanted one of the items of clothing he'd actually managed to hang up?

It was another few hours while he looked for a corkscrew. They'd just clinked their glasses together when the phone rang.

I figured it was probably his wife, calling to tell him all the cute things the kids had done today.

"I'd better get it," said the family man. He obviously thought it was probably his wife, too. "You never know, it could be an emergency. Lucy may have broken another fingernail."

It wasn't his wife.

"The garage has brought the car back," he informed Lil. "It's downstairs. Come on, let's go to that Italian place Hal was talking about. We can have the wine when we get back."

I couldn't believe my luck. Talk about being saved by the bell.

I gave them fifteen minutes to get out and away from the travel lodge, and then I limped out of my hiding place. I didn't really want to run into Mr Wolsky if I could help it, so I went out of one of the fire exits at the back.

Near-death experiences (or, in my case, near-total-disaster experiences) definitely put things in perspective. Normally, I would've been worried that Ella had given up and left me to walk home. But I was so relieved to get free before the next morning (especially without being caught) that I didn't care if I had to crawl home on my knees.

Even though I know how loyal, steadfast and true Ella is, it was a mega-pleasant surprise to see that her car was in front of the diner, just where it was supposed to be. But she wasn't alone. Sam was beside her, turned in his seat, chatting to Ella, but with his eyes on the hotel. He nodded when he saw me as soon as I came around the building.

Both of them were out of the car before I reached it.

"Are you all right?" cried Ella. "I was worried sick! Do you know what time it is?"

I wasn't even sure what day it was; I felt like I'd been locked in the Black Hole of Calcutta for months.

"What the hell happened to you?" Sam has a less maternal nature than Ella. "We thought you'd been arrested."

"Except that one side of my body's gone numb and I've lopped twenty years off my life, I'm fine," I said to Ella. I looked at Sam. "What are you doing here? I thought you were on vacation from me."

"I called him," said Ella. "I didn't know what else to do."

"So naturally I came running." He gave me a wry smile. "I don't like long vacations. The peace and quiet when I'm not speaking to you drive me nuts."

"Let's get moving." I threw myself into the back seat like a girl who's been floating on the ocean on a plank for the last three days would throw herself onto dry land. "All will be revealed when we get out of here."

I gave them the basic outline of my story – our heroine hides in closet; our heroine is so exhausted from her hours of sweat and toil that she falls asleep; girl wakes up to find herself trapped in closet by amorous couple – while Ella tore out of the parking lot and down the road like we were in a cop show.

"I told you it was a crazy idea," said Ella when I'd finished.

Sam looked at me over the back of his seat. "You know, you really should try getting in touch with reality once in a while, Lola. Just for a change."

I took exception to this comment. If anything, I was a lot more in touch with reality than I'd been before I got stuck in Charley Hottle's closet – now I knew that Mr Family Values might not believe in extramarital sex for anybody else, but he definitely believed in it for himself.

"Snooping," said Sam. "Now you've added snooping to your list of talents."

"I wasn't snooping, I was waiting. If that guy hadn't come in—"

"All I can say is, thank God you weren't caught," said Ella. "If it hadn't been for—"

"Well, I wasn't caught." You can't worry about something that didn't happen, can you? "Next time will be different."

"Next time?" Sam was shaking his head as if it

was on a spring. "Chrissake, Lola, don't you ever get the message? Give up."

The exchange of opinions caused by that comment took us all the way to the Creeks' residence. "I'd love to keep arguing with you," said Sam, "but we're really busy right now. Those rental cars the production company has are all crap. I've got to get some rest."

Ella waited while I got into the front seat.

"You know, Lola," she said as she pulled away from the kerb. "Sam—"

"Never mind Sam," I said. "He's fine. We were just having a discussion."

"No," said Ella, "that's not what—"

"Let's get going." I yawned. "I'm totally wiped. I need to get some rest, too. After all – tomorrow is another day."

[Cue: sigh of a tragic hero – long-suffering but too noble to complain.] "With you it doesn't always seem like that," said Ella.

Reality Meets My Fantasies
Head On

By the next morning my batteries were fully recharged and I was ready to make another (and this time guaranteed successful) attack on Charley Hottle.

"I'm telling you, I've worked it all out," I was saying to Ella as we padded down the hall to get our equipment. "All I have to do is—"

Ella said, "Shhh!"

"What?"

She stopped. "Don't you hear that? It sounds like someone crying."

I listened. I could hear something, but it was so low and muffled that unless you were a dolphin (or Ella) it was hard to tell whether it was someone sobbing or the sewer backing up.

Ella pointed to the supply closet. "It sounds like it's coming from in there."

"Ten bucks says it isn't Mrs Seiser," I whispered. "Which means that it has to be Gracia."

177

"Poor Gracia." Ella's been raised to be polite and not to intrude on someone else's distress. She looked at me. "Should we do something?"

I've pretty much been raised to be polite and not to intrude on someone else's distress, too, but it's something I can overcome when necessary – and in this case it was definitely necessary. Not only did we have to get our work stuff out of the closet, but Gracia was our friend. You don't leave your friend crying amid the cleaning equipment. I went over and knocked gently on the door. "Hello?" I called. "Gracia? Are you all right?"

She opened the door enough to look out, tears streaming down her face.

"Gracia, what's wrong?"

She shook her head. "*Nada. Nada.* I'm all right."

"But you're not all right. You're crying."

Even though it seemed pretty likely that Gracia already knew she was crying, this made her cry even more.

"Let us in," I ordered. I pushed on the door and she stepped back enough to let me and Ella squeeze past her. It was a tight fit.

I put a hand on her shoulder as much in sympathy as because I had to put my hand somewhere. "What's wrong?" I asked again.

Ella took a packet of Kleenex from her pocket.

"*¡Dios mío!*" sobbed Gracia, taking a tissue. "*¡Dios mío! ¡Dios mío!*"

"Aren't you well?" asked Ella. "Have you hurt

178

your back again?"

Shaking her head, Gracia dabbed at her eyes. "*¡Dios mío! ¡Dios mío!*"

"Is it one of the kids?" I guessed. "One of your cousins?"

"*¡Dios mío! ¡Dios mío!*"

"Something that happened back home in Colombia?" ventured Ella. "Has another of your relatives been murdered?"

"*¡Dios mío! ¡Dios mío!*" She was crying so hard it looked like someone had thrown a bucket of water over her face.

"Please," I begged, "you have to calm down. Tell us what happened. Maybe we can help."

Gracia launched herself into an explanation of what happened – in Spanish. Ella got A grades in Spanish in school but it wasn't much help. Gracia didn't speak slowly, clearly and distinctly like Señor Goldblatt.

"*Más despacio, por favor,*" Ella pleaded. "*Más despacio, por favor.*"

Gracia gulped and choked and wiped several thousand tears from her eyes. She started again.

"*Reloj?*" Ella repeated. "Watch? You lost your watch?"

"Watch?" With so many other things on my mind, I'd totally forgotten about the gold Rolex. "What watch?"

Gracia nodded. "Not mine," she snuffled. "*El señor's.* Mrs Seiser says I stole it. She is ending my employment."

179

"But she can't do that! You've worked here for ages." Mrs Seiser complained that "those people" had no loyalty or commitment, but obviously in Mrs Seiser's world loyalty and commitment were a one-way street.

"What señor?" asked Ella.

I said, "Charley Hottle."

Ella snapped around like something on a spring. "What do you mean, 'Charley Hottle'? How do you know whose watch it is?" Her face took on the expression of a girl who's just opened the front door to find a dude in a Halloween mask wielding an axe. "Oh, Lola, you di—"

"Of course I didn't. I'm an actor, Ella, not a thief. But I know who did." And I told her about the guy from the crew putting the Rolex in his pocket.

"But that's terrific!" Ella hugged me. "That's wonderful!" She hugged Gracia. "Lola can tell Mrs Seiser what really happened and you won't lose your job. Everything's going to be all right."

I wasn't exactly jumping up and down with joy myself, though. "You think I should tell Old Boot Face the truth?"

The I-opened-the-wrong-door look was back on Ella's face. "What do you mean, do I think you should tell her the truth?"

I could see my last frail hopes of getting into the movie fade into the stack of toilet paper behind Ella's head. They were moving fast and waving goodbye.

180

"But I'll incriminate myself. I'm not even supposed to be on that floor in the daytime, never mind after I've already gone home."

"Lola is right," croaked Gracia. "She will loose her hob."

I often see Mrs Gerard in Ella, but right then I was seeing Karen Kapok. "So what?" asked Ella.

I didn't want to lose my job. I wanted another crack at Charley Hottle. I wanted to be in the movie. I wanted to go to Carla's party with my head held high and the last laugh rattling around in my throat. I looked from the stern, uncompromising glare of my best friend to Gracia's damp gaze. Bergstrom's wasn't my life; my life was waiting for me (temporarily) in Brooklyn. So what if I lost my job? So what if I didn't get in the movie? So what if Carla Santini humiliated me one last time? It wasn't like my world was going to end. But if Gracia lost her job for stealing she might as well go back to Colombia and let them shoot her.

[Cue: sigh of the doomed hero who knows there's no way to go but forward.] "So better my job than Gracia's."

Ella stood shoulder to shoulder with me while I told Mrs Seiser what I saw. Mrs Seiser stared at me the whole time like a poker player with a winning hand.

"What are you saying?" she asked when I was done.

What had she been listening to? Voices in her head?

"I'm saying Gracia didn't take Mr Hottle's watch," I repeated with superhuman patience. "It was one of the guys in the film crew."

Her lips twitched. "And what did you say you were doing on the second floor after you were supposed to have gone home?"

[Cue: deep breath, Mona Lisa smile and subtle avoidance of eye contact with Ella.] "I told you, I was looking for Gracia. I had a phone number to give her ... a chiropractor ... for her back."

This time it was a Seiser eyebrow that twitched. "Gracia left right after you."

"But I didn't know that. I thought she might still be working."

Mrs Seiser has a way of setting her lips that looks like she's folded her arms across her chest and sniffed. "And you just happened to be in the hallway when this man came out of Mr Hottle's room, pocketing the watch."

"That's right. I noticed it because it was a gold Rolex and I don't see that many of them in my daily life."

Mrs Seiser continued to stare at me like I was a guest trying to sneak a towel out in her suitcase.

I nodded emphatically. "That's exactly what happened."

Old Boot Face smirked. "I'm not so sure. The fact that you've appointed yourself the cleaning staff's union representative wouldn't have anything to do with this, would it, Lola?"

"But I'm telling the truth!" This always happens to me. When I lie, people believe me; and when I tell the truth, they don't.

Mrs Seiser's smile grew into a Cheshire Cat grin. "And why should I take your word over the interests of the hotel?"

"Excuse me?"

"You can't think I'm going to accuse one of our guests of stealing from another guest, can you? I've had enough trouble from these people. And Mr Hottle is an important man."

Ella flared up. "But Gracia's important, too."

"That's right." I stared back into those eyes as cold as a winter night in Norway. "And I don't see why you can't accuse one guest of stealing from another when it happens to be true."

Mrs Seiser's laughter was a pretty rare event, which was probably just as well. "Says *you*."

She didn't want to believe me. Like most people, Mrs Seiser wanted a quiet life. Whereas people with striving, artistic souls want nothing more than to stand beneath the Victoria Falls of the emotions and be washed with experience and passion, people with narrow, bureaucratic souls just want a warm room and an easy time. In the drab, grey world of Mrs Seiser, believing that Gracia stole the Rolex was preferable to accusing one of the movie crew and causing a major scene. Besides, Gracia was expendable. And so, apparently, was I.

"I see no reason to keep you on either," said Mrs Seiser. "You're a lot more trouble than you're worth."

Which I, personally, felt was something you could also say about *her*.

Ella, of course, rose to the occasion like the true sister of my heart and soul that she is.

"Then I have to quit, too," said Ella. "There's no way I'm staying on when you're making a mockery of fairness and justice like this." If Ella had been one of Christ's disciples he would've built his church on her and not Peter.

"So be it," said Mrs Seiser.

I Decide To Take The Law Into My Own Hands

In books and movies and stuff like that, getting fired is always a pretty depressing event (Christmas is cancelled, children cry, mothers wring their hands, men get drunk...), but Ella and I were elated. It was better than finishing school. Instead of no more teachers and no more books, it was no more dirty toilets and unmade beds. I considered it a very major rite of passage into the real world, and to celebrate, Ella and I went bowling with Morty and Sam that night.

But elation is a transient thing, and mine ended when we walked into the alleys. There was a woman mopping up spilled soda in the foyer. She was in her forties and she looked really tired. Even though she didn't physically resemble Gracia (except for having a nose, two eyes and a mouth), she reminded me of her. Here she was in her middle years, with nothing to look forward to but cleaning up other people's messes until she was too old to lift a bucket of water. But Gracia didn't even have that to look forward to any more. My good mood went belly up like a bunch of bombed fish. I'd been so happy because I'd stood up for the poor and oppressed like Robin Hood, but for all I'd accomplished I might as well have burned down Sherwood Forest.

I knocked over two pins all evening.

"What's the matter with you?" Sam asked as we sat down in the snack bar. "You couldn't have hit a truck if it was parked at the end of the alley."

"I can't stop thinking about Gracia and Old Boot Face." [Cue: the sigh of the warrior who has fought the good fight and been beaten.] "It's preying on my mind."

Sam put his arm around me. "But you did the right thing." He shook his head in wonder, like a boy who's just rubbed two sticks together and actually made a fire. "You are the darndest girl I've ever known."

Ella unwrapped her straw. "You should be proud of yourself," said Ella. "You stood up for what was right."

Morty picked up a wodge of nachos. "Which is an even bigger deal than standing up to the Santini."

The thing was, I couldn't exactly claim a triumphant victory, could I?

"But Gracia still lost her job. And that's not fair."

Sam passed me the fries. "Maybe not, but at least you tried your best."

I stared at the pile of potatoes more or less drowning in ketchup, imagining Gracia and her children sitting down to a simple meal of bread and water. There would be candles burning (because the electricity had been turned off) and they would bow their heads as they thanked God for even this paltry fare; it was better than being shot.

"And she'll get another job," said Morty. "Cleaning is a growth industry around here."

I shook my head. "No she won't. How's she going to get a job without a reference?"

Ella agreed. "Especially if Mrs Seiser spreads it around that Gracia was stealing."

And she'd do it, too. A woman who counts the toilet rolls every morning and evening is a woman with a mean, unpleasant nature. An image of Gracia (barefoot and wrapped in bin bags for warmth) trudging through the snows of New Jersey came into my mind. *Please...* she begged. *I have children... I need work... I am not a thief...* One-by-one, the doors of Dellwood slammed shut in her face. *That's not what Mrs Seiser says!*

"Maybe my dad can help," offered Sam. "We could use someone to clean the office – and he knows just about everybody in town. If he puts in a good word for her—"

"My mom cleans her own house," cut in Morty, "but she's got friends who don't. Maybe she could get Gracia a couple of jobs."

[Cue: grateful, bittersweet smile.] "It's not enough. I've got to clear Gracia's name."

187

"And how are you going to do that?" asked Ella.

I stirred my drink with my straw. "Don't worry," I said, "I'll think of something."

Sam and Morty groaned.

It took me a couple of days to realize what I had to do (for which I blame all the trauma I'd been through recently). I had to go to Charley Hottle and tell him everything in a calm, direct way. A great actor has to have ambition of course, but ruthless ambition is as unattractive in thespians as it is in politicians and gangsters. So even if I still had the most infinitesimal chance of being in the movie (which even I could see was pretty unlikely), making sure the truth was heard and clearing Gracia's name were much more important than that. The good news was that I didn't have to rely on subterfuge or scheming for this; I could go right up to him and make him listen.

Ella didn't need any convincing at all. She was as concerned about Gracia as I was.

"I can't believe I'm saying this, but for once I think you're right," said Ella. "And anyway, there's nothing to lose, is there?"

"Exactly." I looked in the rearview mirror again.

We were in front of the diner, parked so that we could see any car entering the travel lodge parking lot without turning around. Even though it was too late for Old Boot Face to be on duty, we didn't want to be spotted by the night manager, who would have been warned against us, so we'd taken Mrs Gerard's car and were disguised as suburban housewives (we'd also taken Mrs Gerard's clothes). As soon as Charley Hottle rolled up, I would leap from the car and grab him before he got into Bergstrom's. I'd tell him the truth about being in his room and seeing that guy take his watch and how Gracia's life had been ruined (again) because she'd lost her job. Telling the truth never really seems to do it for me, but at least I had Right on my side.

"But I think we can be more positive than that," I went on. "I mean, there's a really good chance this could work. He has seven children of his own. He's bound to be sympathetic to Gracia's plight."

"He isn't Father of the Year though, is he?" asked Ella.

"Just because he's an adulterer doesn't mean he's going to want to see Gracia's children living on the street." I figured I could have him in tears if he gave me half a chance.

Ella jumped so suddenly she hit the horn. "Quick!" she hissed. "Here he comes."

The purple people carrier was pulling into a space near the front door. I gave myself one brief check in the mirror – sunglasses straight, hat in place, make-up subdued – hooked Mrs Gerard's beige summer bag over my shoulder and leapt from the car.

I was standing right there when he opened the door.

[Cue: direct eye contact and dignified bearing.]

"Mr Hottle," I said, "I really have to talk to you."

"Not now." He moved to get out, but I was blocking his way like Joan of Arc facing the English.

"I'm afraid this can't wait. It's extremely important. The health and well-being of young children are at stake."

"Look, I've had a long day." He glanced at the clock on the dashboard. "And I'm meeting someone here in a few minutes. If you want an autograph, fine, but I don't have time for an interview."

"I don't want an interview. I want to talk to you." I stood firm and tall. "It's about Gracia."

Charley Hottle said, "Who?"

"Gracia. The woman who made your bed and cleaned your toilet. The second-floor maid."

But (as I already knew to my cost) busy, important men aren't interested in maids.

Charley Hottle turned to the driver. "Give me a hand here, will you, Ben?"

Ben jumped out of the driver's seat. I braced myself between the door and the frame.

"Mr Hottle, please. You've got to listen. Gracia lost her job because your watch was stolen. But she didn't take it, Mr Hottle. I swear it. I know who did."

"Don't you understand English? I don't have time for this now."

"But it's important. A family's life is being ruined. Tiny children with doe-eyes and dark curls are being turned into the street where they'll have to survive on scraps of food they find in the rubbish bins."

Ben put a very unfatherly hand on my shoulder. "Come on. You heard Mr Hottle. Why don't you go home before you find yourself in serious trouble?"

"Please, Mr Hottle. Please, please, please! You have to listen to me." I would've clasped my hands in prayer if I could've let go of the door.

Not that holding on did me any good.

Ben took his hand from my shoulder and lifted me into the air.

"Let's just back off a little here."

Charley Hottle scuttled past me, heading for Bergstrom's.

"You let go of her!" Ella came charging across the parking lot like the cavalry across the Great Plains. "My father's a lawyer!" she screamed. "A very good lawyer! Unless you want to end up in court you'd better put my friend down!"

I don't think it was the threat so much as the distraction of seeing a woman in a pink summer suit, clutching a floppy picture hat with roses on it to her head, running towards him that made him release me.

"What the hell—"

"I want your name and address!" Ella slowed to a brisk walk, taking a notebook and pen from Mrs Gerard's tasteful straw bag as she neared him. She's not her mother's daughter for nothing.

I had already bolted after Charley Hottle. He had his hand on the door of Bergstrom's, but I didn't care.

"Mr Hottle! Mr Hottle!" I threw myself in front of him. "You have to listen to me! I saw who took your watch. I can describe him. I can pick him out of a line-up."

"I'm warning you. Get out of my way."

"But I saw him! It was the guy you sent to your room to get your notebook. I saw him put it in his pocket!"

He was surprised that I knew about the notebook.

"And how could you know a thing like that?"

"I told you. Because I saw him! I saw him put it in his pocket."

"And where were you when you saw this?"

"In your closet."

People are always blanching in old novels, but this was the first time I'd ever seen someone actually do it right in front of me. His face went the colour of a peeled nut.

"You were where?"

"In your closet. I wasn't doing anything – I just wanted to talk to you so I was waiting—"

It was beginning to look like his blood was draining out through his feet. "You were waiting for me in my closet? How long were you in there? Is this some kind of set-up? Just who the hell are you?"

This was my moment to restore order and get

his attention by letting him know that I knew about his girlfriend and that he could consider me a friend. "Don't worry, Mr Hottle," I assured him, "I won't tell anybody what I overheard. I—"

"Won't tell anybody? Won't tell anybody what? Are you threatening me?"

I was about to say that of course I wasn't threatening him, I just wanted to talk, when, in a pretty graphic and aggressive way, all hell broke loose.

Ella and Ben joined us, arguing amongst themselves. (I'd never heard her scream so much; Mrs Gerard would've fainted on the spot.)

And Mrs Seiser loomed on the other side of the glass doors, looking like the Hotel Manager Possessed by Demons.

What's she doing here? screamed my brain. *She's supposed to be at home terrorizing Mr Seiser.*

I was so surprised to see her that I jumped back from the door.

"What in God's name's going on here?" shrieked Mrs Seiser. "Let go of this man! He's a guest in this hotel!" I had this cloth doll when I was little that was Little Red Riding Hood if you held it one way, and the Big Bad Wolf if you turned it inside out. Mrs Seiser did a pretty good impersonation of that doll. When she was screaming at me she was the Big Bad Wolf, but when she turned to Charley Hottle she was Little Red Riding Hood on her very best behaviour. "Mr Hottle," she purred, "are you all right? You don't

193

have to worry, I called the police."

That was the last clear sentence I actually heard because everybody started shouting at once (mainly at me – though, for my part, I concentrated on Charley Hottle). And then the police arrived, with their lights and siren going. Everybody came out of the diner and cars pulled over to the shoulder to watch (anything bigger than someone going through a stop sign is pretty exciting in Dellwood).

The cops managed to get everyone to stop screaming.

Officer Pintelli took out his notebook. "All right, I want you to tell me what's going on – one at a time." He aimed his pen at Mrs Seiser. "Starting with you."

But it wasn't Mrs Seiser who spoke next. It was someone behind us.

"Chrissake, Lola," he said. "Now what've you done?"

We all turned around.

Charley Hottle looked like he was going to hug him. "Sam! Do you know this lunatic?" He was pointing at me.

"Yeah," said Sam. "This is Lola. She's the girl I was telling you about."

Into The Future
– Forget The Past

The words "I hope you learned something from this" have been part of the constant background music of my life for as long as I can remember. Now was no exception.

"I hope you learned something from this," said Sam.

"I hope you learned something from this," said Ella.

"I hope you finally learned something from this," said Karen Kapok.

Well I'd definitely learned something this time. I'd learned that a lot of those old sayings that seem so trite and boring actually have a lot of truth in them. Especially the one about being your own worst enemy.

"I was going to tell you about Charley Hottle coming into the garage the night you decided to stalk Bret Fork," said Sam.

Hell hath no fury like a grease-monkey scorned.

I said, "Oh."

Charley Hottle knew the value of a good mechanic because his father had been one, so when the people carrier kept stalling on him, he took it to Creek and Son himself. Mr Magnolia recommended them. Sam and Charley Hottle bonded while looking under the bonnet together, the way men do. Charley Hottle said Sam would've been a lot better for Bret Fork's part than Bret Fork, but in his opinion the world needed more gifted mechanics than it did mediocre actors.

Sam gave me one of his who's-been-riding-the-clutch-again looks. "My dad even tried to introduce you to him." He made it sound like an accusation.

I don't see how I could've known that. I'm highly intuitive like all great actors, but I'm not psychic. I said, "Oh."

It wasn't chance that brought Mr Creek to the Dellwood Diner that morning as anyone would have supposed, it was a power breakfast with Charley Hottle. Since all the rented vehicles had problems, Charley Hottle wanted to get to the head of the line and he figured the best way to do that was to buy Mr Creek his fried eggs and hash browns.

"And I tried to tell you, too," said Ella. "The night we rescued you from Bergstrom's, but you wouldn't listen."

It was Sam's idea to deliver Charley Hottle's car to the travel lodge after Ella called him the night I hid in the closet. Sam thought that if he could talk to him he might find out what had happened to me. When he realized Charley Hottle hadn't seen me, he figured that, unlikely as it seemed, there was a chance I was still in the room. He was just about to go looking for me when I came out of the building.

I could see that I hadn't exactly been helping myself by being a little single-minded and alienating my closest allies. I said, "Oh."

On the other hand, in a way I was also my own best friend.

Charley Hottle had been meeting Sam the night I confronted him in the parking lot (the night described by the local paper as Bust-up at Bergstrom's). Sam wanted to talk to him about me. He said he thought that after the way I'd stood up for Gracia I deserved some help.

So after all the trauma and emotional upheaval had settled down, Charley Hottle invited Ella, Sam and me to go to Triolo's with him for supper.

We laughed a lot about Ella's and my attempts to get in the movie (especially the part where we staggered over the cliff like soldiers who just found out the war's been over for forty years).

Then we laughed some more about our adventures in the cleaning industry (especially the part where I fell asleep in the closet).

Charley Hottle looked from me to Sam. "She's exactly as you described her." He sounded really surprised.

But I had been totally right about one thing. After everything had been explained to him (and Mr Triolo's aubergine parmigiana had worked its magic), Charley Hottle acted like a man of reason and generosity.

"Don't worry," said Charley Hottle. "I'll have my watch back tomorrow. And before my ex-employee leaves, he and I will have a talk with Mrs Seiser. You can tell Gracia to expect a call to come back to work *and* an apology."

I couldn't have been happier if I'd just won an Oscar. Not that Gracia needed the job at Bergstrom's any more. Between Morty's mom and Sam's dad, she was already in full-time employment. But it meant she could tell Mrs Seiser to take her uniform and her nametag and her cleaning cart and shove it down a toilet.

Charley Hottle pushed his empty plate away. "There's one other thing I'd like to do." He looked from me to Ella. "I'd like to give you both a little spot in the movie. We need a couple of girls to walk past Lucy Rio in the high school corridor."

Ella smiled. "Really?"

But I didn't smile. I was surprised to realize that this announcement didn't exactly make jubilation race through my heart.

Sam caught the look on my face. "Now what?"

"Well…" I shrugged. "I don't know if I really want to be in the movie any more."

"What?" Charley Hottle was surprised, too. "I thought you'd be happy. I thought that was what you wanted."

"It was," I said. "It is. It's just that..."

Charley Hottle, Ella and Sam all said, "It's just what?"

It was the hypocrisy. If Charley Hottle wasn't always going on about family values and his kids and his wife I really wouldn't care what he did in his spare time. I mean, it wouldn't be any of my business, would it? But he was always going on about it. He was like that TV preacher who told people what a major sin adultery is, and then they caught him with a prostitute. I figured that if I accepted a part in the movie I'd be saying it's all right to say one thing and do something else.

I shrugged. "It's just that I feel uncomfortable." I kept my eyes on the candle in the middle of the table. "You know, because of your girlfriend."

Ella sighed. "Oh... I get it."

Charley Hottle turned to Sam. "Now what's she talking about?"

Sam said, "Umph." He looked like he was hoping the floor was going to collapse and take him with it.

"You know..." I was mumbling. "The woman you had in your room."

Charley Hottle turned to me. He was half-smiling, like maybe I was making a joke he didn't understand. "You mean my wife?"

Ella looked hopeful. "That was your wife?"

"Of course it was my wife."

But I wasn't going to start ringing the bells of joy

just yet. "I thought your wife's called Tamara."

I'd expected Charley Hottle to get all angry and defensive, but instead he grinned. "It is Tamara." He gave me a wink. "Maybe you'd like to take a wild guess at what my nickname for her is."

"Oh, let me." Sam shot me a you-forgot-to-check-the-oil-again look. "It couldn't be Lil, could it?"

"So is it OK now?" Charley Hottle asked after we'd all stopped laughing. "Do we have a deal?"

I said we had a deal.

Sam wanted to know if being friends with Charley Hottle and getting the part and everything meant that we didn't have to go to Carla's party.

I said no.

"Ella and Morty are going with us. And besides, everybody's going to be there. You can't possibly think I'm going to miss my last chance to wipe the smile from the Santini's face when she sees me being all pally with Charley Hottle. I've been waiting my whole life for this."

"You haven't known Carla for your whole life."

"Well it seems like I have."

There was a communal gasp inside the Karmann Ghia as Carla's house came into view.

Just in case you weren't sure which mansion belonged to the Santinis, coloured floodlights waved gently across the New Jersey sky from the front lawn. There was a woman done up as Marilyn Monroe checking invitations at the door

200

and a man dressed as Charlie Chaplin telling people where to park.

"Chrissake," muttered Sam. "Doesn't she know there are people starving on this planet?"

"I'm surprised she doesn't have photographers lined up," said Morty.

"She's really surpassed herself this time, hasn't she?" said Ella.

I sighed. "It's exactly what you'd expect from someone who's never gone without anything except a soul."

"How long do we have to stay?" asked Sam as he came to a stop at the end of the street. He'd agreed to come, but he wasn't going to be too gracious about it.

"For God's sake, we haven't even got out of the car yet."

"I'd be really happy if we could do that straight away," Morty grunted. "I think I may be permanently crippled."

"I don't know why I bothered ironing this dress," complained Ella. "It looks like I slept in it."

Sam still hadn't taken the keys from the ignition or made any movement to open his door. "So how long?"

"No more than an hour." I pulled the handle on the passenger side and more or less rolled out. "Just long enough to mingle a little and bid the Santini a fond farewell."

"Right," said Sam. "But if you're not ready in an hour I'm leaving without you."

The Hollywood theme was continued inside the house. All the waiters were dressed as movie stars, too, and Mr Santini was wearing a beret like an old-time director.

Morty and Sam went off to find a quiet corner where they could play backgammon until the hour was up.

Ella and I mingled.

"Gosh," said Ella as we fought our way through the merry throngs. "She really did invite everyone, didn't she?"

"Not everyone." I didn't see Charley Hottle – or anyone else from the movie for that matter. How was Carla going to see me being all pally with Charley Hottle if he wasn't there?

Ella was less than sympathetic. "Does that mean we can leave?"

"No."

Most of the revellers were in the back yard. Music was playing through a sophisticated sound system that seemed to be embedded in the trees and more floodlights wafted over the patio and the pool.

Never let it be said that Ella has no talent for stating the obvious.

"I can't see her," said Ella.

Neither did I. "That's funny… It's not like Carla to hide herself away."

We went back into the house.

There were at least fifty people dancing in the living room, but none of them was related to Mr Santini.

Nor was Dellwood's reigning monarch in the games room (ping-pong, pinball, video games and shuffleboard) or the dining room (more food than most of the world sees in a year) either.

"Isn't the hour up yet?" grumbled Ella as we reached the entertainment room. "I'm exhausted. It's like trying to get through the mall on Christmas Eve."

"No. We go nowhere until I've accomplished my mission." I opened the door.

The room was packed with people, and dark except for the light coming from the enormous TV screen that filled almost an entire wall, but I spotted Carla immediately. She was sitting in the middle of the sofa, flanked by the witches of Dellwood on either side. Everyone was watching the screen.

"I don't get it," whispered Ella. "What's going on?"

Voices I'd barely heard at the time because I was kind of busy came back to me. *You mean Dellwood's answer to Fellini...? The last time I saw her she was taking pictures of Lucy... I think she was going to shoot Bret eating his lunch...*

"It looks like Carla's made a movie."

What I did on My Summer Vacation.

A great actor has to trust her instincts, but my instincts were taking a break right then because instead of backing out of the room I stayed where I was, riveted to the spectacle unfolding before my wondering eyes.

There was Charley Hottle waving his hands around like he was besieged by a swarm of flies. There was Lucy Rio sitting on a motorcycle. There was Bret Fork talking on his cell phone. And in almost every scene there was Carla, smiling like she'd just invented air. Alma must've been in charge of the camera.

Carla really has to be a witch, there's no other explanation for what happened next.

The image on the screen froze and she suddenly turned around, as though she knew we were there all the time.

"Lola!" she cried.

Everyone else in the room turned around too.

"I was afraid you were going to miss the best part. It's just coming up."

Ella pulled on my arm. "Let's go."

My instincts weren't just taking a break; they were asleep at the wheel. Instead of bolting I said, "I just wanted to say how sorry I am we didn't see you on the set this summer. Charley Hottle said you made a great waiter in the scene in the diner."

Alma, Marcia and Tina all tittered, but everyone else stayed silent, watching us the way you'd watch a gunfight.

"Maybe we didn't see you because you weren't actually in the movie like you said," suggested Alma.

[Cue: raising of chin and confident smile.] "Oh, we were there. You'll see when it comes out. We're in the—"

Carla cut me off. "Of course they were there, Al." She pressed the remote and the movie started playing again. "And here's the proof."

I gave a small, puzzled laugh. "Bret Fork eating a sandwich?"

Carla waved her diamond bracelet in my direction. "It's should be right after this."

The camera panned around the canteen at the other actors and crew having lunch and glided back to Bret, lifting a can of soda to his mouth. I knew what should be right after this.

"Oh my God…" whispered Ella. She knew too.

It was Ella and me being marched off the set. I could only hope that she was too far away to pick up the short but pithy lecture Mr Muscle gave us about not getting any closer to the production than Ottawa after this.

"Lola, let's go," hissed Ella.

I didn't move.

Why not? Was it because I was mature enough to understand that what Carla had said in my dream was true: you can run, but you can never hide?

No, that wasn't it. I mean, I was mature enough to understand that of course, but that wasn't the reason I didn't bolt for the door. I looked at Carla, smiling at me like the cat that's just swallowed every fish in the lake. And at Marcia, Alma and Tina, smug as the devil's own henchmen. And at the rest of the kids in the room, one eye on the TV and one eye on me. And I really didn't care what any of them thought or believed. They weren't my friends and they weren't people I respected. I'd had more kindness shown to me by Gracia, who had plenty of reason to resent me, coming in and doing for fun what she did to survive. A disaster to Carla was breaking a fingernail. A disaster for Gracia was having her husband gunned down or losing her job. Working at Bergstrom's had taught me a lot about the real world, and I didn't think that Carla Santini had anything to do with it any more.

"Oh, I know what's coming." I was one beat ahead of the Carla Santini show. "This is where Ella and I were thrown off the set, isn't it?"

And there we were, firmly in the grip of Mr Muscle, being shoved towards the road.

Mine was a free and easy laugh.

"Watch this!" I cried. "This is where I trip over a cable. Remember that, Ella? I nearly brought down the producer."

One of the reasons I love Ella is because even though she worries a lot and dislikes serious confrontations, she always rises to the occasion.

Ella laughed too. "I thought you'd broken your ankle, the way you screamed."

[Cue: more laughter from the gathered throng.]

"How come you look like that?" asked someone. "You look like you'd been swimming."

"With sharks," added someone else.

"We'd just walked along the shore and climbed up the cliff." The Santini glass-bells laugh had nothing on my laugh. It sounded like wind chimes

206

made by Tiffany.

There were a few hoots of "Really?" and "You're kidding."

"Well there was no other way to get up there, was there? The road was blocked for miles."

Only Carla and the coven weren't laughing along.

"I thought you said you had a part in the movie," said Carla with this-cake-is-poisoned sweetness.

"That's right, you said you had a part." If all else fails, Alma could always become a professional echo chamber. "So why did you have to climb up the cliff?"

"You didn't really believe I had a part, did you?" I gave Alma a pitying look. "I was just kidding. But then of course things got a little out of hand." I turned to the crowd. "You want to hear what happened? It's a lot more interesting than Carla's movie, believe me."

I can't help feeling that acting's gain could be something of a loss to the world of storytelling. If there'd been any aisles in the Santinis' entertainment room I would've had my audience rolling in them with my many adventures of trying to get Charley Hottle's attention.

"And that," I said when my story finally came to its happy end, "is how I became a Hollywood star!"

[Cue: wild applause and the slamming of the door as Carla stalked from the room.]

*   *   *

After we drove Morty and Ella home Sam came back to my house with me.

"You never fail to amaze me," said Sam. "I can't believe you actually told everybody the truth for a change."

I sat down next to him on the couch. "When I became a woman, I put away childish things," I said.

"I hope that doesn't mean me," said Sam.

I said of course it didn't. It meant Carla Santini. I said I was depending on him to pick me up from Brooklyn every weekend.

"Thanks," said Sam. "It's really nice to be appreciated." He wanted to know what would happen if Charley Hottle gave me a bigger part in his next movie and I had to move to California. Did that mean I wouldn't need him any more?

I said I figured a great mechanic could work anywhere.